W9-BHB-713

SACAGAWEA

★ ★ ★ ★ ★ ★ ★ ★ ★ ★ ★ ★

Name: Sacagawea

Born: c. 1788

Died: c. 1812

Position: Explorer

Career Highlights:

- Was the translator for the Lewis and Clark expedition, which set out to find a route to the Pacific Ocean

Interesting Facts:

- She was the daughter of a Shoshone chief
- During one stop along the journey, she was reunited with her brother who she hadn't seen since childhood

★ ★ ★ ★ ★ ★ ★ ★ ★ ★ ★ ★

SACAGAWEA

HISTORY'S★ ★ALL-STARS

SACAGAWEA

By **Flora Warren Seymour**
Illustrated by **Robert Doremus**

ALADDIN
New York London Toronto Sydney New Delhi

ALADDIN

An imprint of Simon & Schuster Children's Publishing Division
1230 Avenue of the Americas, New York, NY 10020
This Aladdin edition December 2014

For information about special discounts for bulk purchases, please contact
Simon & Schuster Special Sales at 1-866-506-1949 or business@simonandschuster.com.
Cover designed by Laura Lyn DiSiena
Designed by Mike Rosamilia
The text of this book was set in Adobe Caslon Pro.
Manufactured in the United States of America 1114 FFG
2 4 6 8 10 9 7 5 3 1
Library of Congress Catalog Card Number 2014933327
ISBN 978-1-4814-1500-2 (hardcover)
ISBN 978-1-4814-1499-9 (paperback)
ISBN 978-1-4814-1501-9 (eBook)

The name "Sacagawea" has been pronounced in a number of different ways, but the author prefers Sah-kah′gah-way′a as nearest to the way the Native Americans say it.

★ ILLUSTRATIONS ★

Full Pages

Numerous smaller illustrations

★ CONTENTS ★

SACAGAWEA

BIRD GIRL
IN HER NEST

SACAGAWEA CAME OUT of the tepee into the bright sunlight. Her black hair hung about her bare shoulders. Her eyes were brown and so was her skin. An Indian girl of the Shoshone tribe, she was about seven years old.

Her mother was sitting on the ground in front of the tepee.

"What are you doing, Mother?" the girl asked.

"Use your eyes, Bird Girl," said her mother. "Let them answer your questions." She shook out the deerskin on which she was working. It was almost shapeless, but Bird Girl could see that it looked like a soft slipper.

"Oh, I see!" Bird Girl said. "Big Brother's moccasins!"

"I am mending them," her mother explained.

"Where is he going?"

Travels Fast—he was several years older than Sacagawea—had come up and was listening.

"Hunting," he said proudly.

Sacagawea opened her brown eyes wide. Hunting! That meant he was almost grown-up. She felt a bit envious.

"Where are you going? When will you start? May I go, too?"

Travels Fast laughed. "How can I answer three questions at once?" he asked teasingly. "No, hunting trips are not for girls," he went on. "You will be fast asleep when I start off in that direction."

He waved his hand toward one of the rocky hills. These hills were all around the valley where the tepees, or skin tents, of the tribe were. The valley was high up in the Rocky Mountains, in what is now the state of Wyoming. But this was in 1794, long before Wyoming became state. At that time the Shoshone had never even heard of the United States, which was a very new country. Indeed, no one of the whole tribe had ever seen a white man.

"Oh-h-h!" Sacagawea nodded. "The sun comes from behind that hill every morning. Where does the sun start from?"

"Much farther away than that hill, I think," Travels Fast told her.

"Beyond many hills," said Grandmother, who had been listening.

"I want to go see it get up," said Bird Girl.

"It is much too far away," Grandmother

told her. "When we go to hunt the buffalo we go off in that direction. Many days we travel, but still we do not reach the tepee where the sun lives. It is always farther away."

Grandmother saw the disappointment in Bird Girl's face. "Here is something for you to do," she said. She took up a round piece of skin on which she had been working. She had been making slits around it, near the edge.

"If you can finish this properly," she said, "it will be a nice bag for your belongings." She laid it out on the flattened log on which she often worked.

"See how I have made these narrow slits? There are a few more to make, and you must be careful not to let them come out to the edge. When they are finished I will show you how to thread in these two long strings of leather."

Bird Girl took it eagerly, and with Grandmother's sharp stiletto—a kind of pointed knife made from a buffalo bone—she began to cut away at the few holes that were left to do.

"I know what this will be," she thought to herself. "My doll is going to be a medicine man, like Old Man, and cure sick people with her chants. Only I suppose Quiet Child will be a medicine *woman* instead. And in this bag I shall gather all the things for her to make medicine with, to make charms and call out in the dances." It made her laugh to think of her dolly chanting and dancing. Quiet Child was made of a soft piece of deerskin, stuffed with dried grass. Her eyes and nose and mouth were marked with charcoal.

Grandmother looked at Bird Girl, smiling to herself, and saw that she had forgotten her disappointment that she could not go with her brother. But Sacagawea did not forget so quickly. She had made up her mind that if Brother could go hunting, she could go, too.

"I know where to pick berries and how to dig roots," she said to herself. "And I know which ones are good to eat and which will make me sick. I can go to see where the sun rises."

But she did not say this aloud. She worked quietly and soon all the slits were made. Not once did the bone knife slide out of her hand and cut through to the edge! That would have spoiled the bag, she knew.

Then Grandmother showed her how to wind in the strips. She drew them up, puckering the skin together, and there was a fine bag, to be sure! It would hold a lot of things for Quiet Child— pretty sticks and bright stones and maybe a bone. The bone would be a charm, for everybody knew that some bones had magical powers.

"I shall find something for it this very night," Bird Girl decided. "I shall watch when Big Brother goes, and follow him!"

But when evening came and she had eaten her share of the food Mother prepared for them, Sacagawea began to feel sleepy. She thought she would close her eyes for just a little while. Before she knew it she was fast asleep. She did not hear Big Brother when he went off for his first hunt.

It was still dark when Sacagawea woke up. She could scarcely see, but not far away was the skin with which Travels Fast covered himself when he slept. It was all in a pile, but there was no boy under the heap. His bow and arrows were gone, too. He always kept them near him while he slept.

Sacagawea put out her hand and felt Quiet Child, propped against the side of the tepee.

The new bag was beside her, just where it had been left when she went to sleep.

How long had Brother been gone? And how could she get away without awakening Grandmother, who always slept near the entrance to the tepee?

Slowly and carefully she crept toward the opening. She held her breath.

Grandmother moved a little and made a sharp sound. Bird Girl kept perfectly still. She hoped that she would look just like the dark tepee wall, and just as motionless.

Then Grandmother was quiet again, and sleeping. Sacagawea crept past her as carefully and quietly as she could, lifted the flap and came out into the cool darkness.

It was not yet morning. The stars were still shining, and twinkled down at her.

Over by the eastern hill the sky looked a little

lighter, and Sacagawea thought it would not be long until morning.

Brother must have been gone a long time. Would she be able to catch up with him?

Away she went as fast as her feet could go. She did not have any moccasins, and sometimes the stones cut her bare feet.

She had never tried to climb a hill so high and so steep as this one. She scrambled from one rock to another. Once she slipped and scraped some skin off her ankle. But she kept going.

She felt as if she had been on her way for a whole night and day, instead of just part of one. And now, above her, there were streaks of light that told her before long the sun would be coming into sight. "I must hurry faster," she panted.

Just then something pretty caught her eye. It was a bright red feather that had dropped from the breast of a bird.

"This is for Quiet Child's medicine bundle," Bird Girl said. "It will bring good luck."

She held it in her hand as she hurried on.

At last she reached the top of the hill. All she could see was one hill after another, with valleys in between. She could not count them all.

"How big the world is!" said Bird Girl. "I did not dream that it reached so far."

And a long way off, beyond the highest of all the hills, was the top of a golden circle. The sun was coming up!

"It would take many, many days to travel to that hill," thought Bird Girl. "I won't reach the sun's home this morning." She began to feel discouraged.

And now she began to feel hungry, too. While she had been hurrying to reach the top of the hill she had not thought of looking for food.

She looked around her. Not one bush had any berries on it.

She remembered how the young horses chewed the bark of the small cottonwood trees. But cottonwood trees grew by running water, and she had come far above the stream near the Shoshone tepees. Farther down the hillside she could see a running brook. Water would taste good to her now.

So down through the underbrush she went. How good the cool, clear water felt! And there beside the little stream was a bush with beautiful, juicy red berries. She stuck her red feather in her hair so that she could pick the berries with both hands.

This was a good breakfast. She was sorry she had not found Brother and learned how to hunt. And she was disappointed because the sun's home must be so very, very far away.

She had found out that the world was very large, with many hills and valleys. She had looked up at the wide blue sky with its soft white clouds. She felt very small and a bit afraid to be all alone in such a wide country.

Now, down in the valley where the little brook ran, she somehow felt safer. But it must be time to go home. Brother would be on his way back by this time.

But where was home? From the hilltop she had been able to see the camp of the Shoshone.

However, coming down to the stream she had lost sight of it. How could she find it again? She started in what she thought was the right direction.

On and on she went. Still she could not see the camp. Little birds cheeped and hopped about. Up in the trees others sang their morning songs. None of them told her how to find her way.

"I am a bird girl," she said to herself, "but I can't understand their talk and ask them the way home. And I can't fly, either." Her feet were sore by this time, and the bushes had scratched her.

Grandmother had told her, "Brave girls do not cry." She remembered this, but now and then a tear came into the corner of her eye and started to roll down her cheek. She would dash it away with her hand and wink hard to keep another from following.

"If I were really a bird," she thought, "I'd fly right over these horrid old rocks. I can't, so I think I'll sit down and rest for a while."

She sat down, feeling very lonely. At first it was hard to keep more tears from coming, but pretty soon her eyes closed, and the tired Bird Girl fell asleep.

"Sister! Bird Girl!"

In her sleep Sacagawea felt someone shaking her by the shoulder. She had been dreaming she was a home. But she opened her eyes in a strange place.

There was Travels Fast beside her, and suddenly she knew she wasn't lost any longer. She smiled up at him happily.

"How *ever* did you get away off here?" he asked her.

"I wanted to see where the sun lives," Bird Girl answered. "I climbed and climbed and climbed, but it's much farther off than I could go. It's farther than I thought it was."

"Indeed it is," said Travels Fast. "Quite too far for a girl. And all alone, too! We are a long way from home, and Mother must be looking for us both. I went farther hunting than I expected to. See this!"

He held up a rabbit and two prairie hens.

"Let's hurry home and eat them," said his sister. "I'm hungry!"

Travels Fast laughed. "So am I."

They walked a long, long way before they came in sight of the Shoshone camp.

How glad Mother was to see them! She put her arms about the tired girl.

She washed Bird Girl's scratched hands and feet and put cool green leaves on them.

"Mother," asked Sacagawea, "why am I a bird girl?"

"Because when you were a baby, like Little Brother, I saw a great beautiful bird fly to the sky, singing. So I named you for it."

"But if I am a bird, why can't I fly?"

"You watch the little birds," Mother said. "Little birds have to learn to hop first, and afterward they may learn to fly. At first they stay very near the nest and the mother bird. It is not safe to go far away alone.

"So you, my Bird Girl, must stay near this nest of ours for a long time yet. Someday you will be able to go faster and farther than you do now, but that will be when you have grown much bigger than you are now."

"And when I have grown up," said Bird Girl, "I shall fly off beyond the hills to see the sun come out of its tepee in the morning."

"Why were you wearing a feather in your hair, like a warrior?" Travels Fast teased her.

"That is for Quiet Child's new bag," his sister answered. She smoothed the red feather carefully and laid it in the bag she had made the day before.

DOWN TO THE RIVER

"THE BIG FISH ARE COMING up the river!" Travels Fast came running to tell them. He had fun so fast he could hardly talk.

A man who had been scouting had just brought this exciting news. Soon all the people in the camp were at work. Mother and Grandmother began to pack all the skins and tools that were inside the tepee, folding the skin robes and making them into neat bundles.

"You may watch Baby Brother," they told Sacagawea. Baby Brother was safely wrapped up

against his cradleboard. Grandmother propped the board against a tree. The brown-eyed baby looked out and laughed at his sister. Sacagawea sat on the ground beside him.

There had been a hungry time for the Shoshone. Father and the other men came in from hunting with scarcely any meat to cook over their fires. Sacagawea had gone with her mother to hunt berries and roots, but they found very few, for most of them had dried up.

So this was good news about the fish. Everyone felt happy and eager to hurry down to the river, where the men would spear the salmon.

Every day they would have a fine feast at the river. If they were lucky and got many, many fish, the women would hang them up to dry, and store the meat away to be brought out when food became scarce again.

Grandmother had told Sacagawea all about

this. Bird Girl could hardly remember the last time they had gone to the river, for she had been very little then.

"I wish I could go with Big Brother," she thought. The boys had all run off to gather in the horses and get them ready. But she must stay with Baby Brother.

He was growing fast. Sometimes he was taken out of his wood and leather cradle so that he could crawl around on a buffalo skin. Soon he would be learning to walk. Then he would spend most of his time out of his cradle.

Sacagawea would have to take care of him more and more. Her best friend, Willow Girl, had a little sister who had just learned to walk, and she was with the two girls most of the time. Her name was Little Grass.

Willow Girl and her sister came up now and sat down under the tree with Sacagawea.

"Everybody is busy," said Bird Girl. "I am busy, too. I have to take care of Baby Brother."

"Mother told me to bring Little Grass over here," said Willow Girl, "and keep her out of the way. They are going to take down our tepee pretty soon."

The tepee houses in which the Shoshone lived were round tents. The framework of poles came together in a peak at the top, where there was an opening so the smoke from the fire could get out. Over the poles were stretched buffalo hides laced together, which formed the walls of the house.

Mother and Grandmother would soon be ready to take their tepee down.

From where they sat, the girls could hear the boys shouting and see them racing about in the corral, or pen, where the horses were kept. It was surrounded by a fence made of cottonwood

posts driven into the ground, close together.
When the boys caught a horse they would tie
it to the fence by a lariat, or long leather rope,
fastened loosely around the horse's neck.

They all watched while Sacagawea's brother
grabbed a horse by the mane and leaped on its
back.

"What fun boys have!" cried Willow Girl.
"I'd like to do that."

"See how he rides!" cried his sister. "Dipping down first on one side and then on the other. He can shoot his arrows, too, from away down there."

"Wonderful!" said Willow Girl. She looked a little envious. "I wish I had a big brother too."

Sacagawea looked toward the village. "Look!" she cried. "Mother and Grandmother have brought everything out. Now they will begin to take our tepee down."

Sure enough, everything inside the tepee had been made into neat bundles and brought outside. Grandmother began to unlace the skins that came together over the entrance. Soon she and Mother had the whole big covering of skin spread out on the ground.

"It takes a lot of skins to make a tepee," Sacagawea said.

"I counted ours once," Willow Girl told her. She held up all the fingers on one hand—five—and three on the other—eight. "All great big buffalo skins, too."

The covering was so heavy that both Mother and Grandmother had to lift together to fold one side over the other. It was even harder for them to fold the covering again.

"See that mended place?" Bird Girl pointed it out. "Brother threw a sharp-pointed stone through it. The snow came through the holes."

"I guess your grandmother scolded him!" Willow Girl laughed.

"Oh, she did!" Sacagawea opened her eyes wide, remembering. "It took her and Mother a long time to mend it."

Now the tepee covering was a neatly folded pile of skins, and Mother and Grandmother began taking down the tall poles.

They laid the poles carefully side by side on the ground. Little Grass kept running up to them, and Willow Girl tried to keep her from getting in the way. "Suppose one should fall on you!" she said to her sister.

But the younger girl did not listen. She clapped her hands and skipped about.

"Look out!" both Sacagawea and Willow Girl cried to her, as one tall white pole came down almost at her feet. Little Grass jumped. She was willing, then, to come back near her sister. Baby Brother laughed at it all. Sacagawea was glad he was in his cradle and she did not have to keep him from running up to where the women were working.

"Next year," Willow Girl said proudly, "I shall help to pack when we travel."

"How do you know?"

"Mother said so."

Sacagawea looked a little sad. Her mother had not said such a thing to her.

"And next year," Willow Girl went on, "your baby brother will be walking around like Little Grass. He will follow you everywhere you go."

"Just the same," said Bird Girl, "I mean to grow all I can, and maybe I can help pack, too. Next year is a long time off, though, isn't it?"

"Yes, there's a warm time like this when the leaves turn green, and then a hotter time when the streams grow smaller. After that comes a cooler time when the leaves turn different colors and fall off the trees.

"Then comes the cold time when we stay in the tepee close to the fire.

"Then at last the leaves come out again and look green and pretty, and more water comes down the hillside in the river. That's the warm time again, and that will be next year."

"That sounds like many sleeps," Sacagawea said.

"It is," answered Willow Girl. "And we will live in different places, too. Now we are going down to the river to get fish. Some other time we'll go far off in the other direction, where the sun comes from."

By now all over the camp the poles were down and were tied together.

Big Brother came riding up on horseback. The horse was dragging some poles that were fastened together in a three-cornered frame.

Sacagawea knew what this was for. She remembered the last time they had moved. But Willow Girl felt that it must all be explained to Little Grass, who looked on with her big brown eyes wide open.

"He's going to carry the tepee away," said Willow Girl. Little Grass nodded her head. Her black hair swung back and forth as she nodded.

They all watched as Mother and Grand-mother put the poles on the three-cornered frame and tied them tightly. On top of them they tied the bundles of skin that were the tepee covering.

"There goes your house," said Willow Girl.

"What happened to the fire?" asked Little Grass.

Mother and Grandmother had put the fire out. On the bare place where the tepee had stood there were just some black stones and gray ashes to show where the fire had been. The three girls went over and poked at them.

Then Sacagawea and Little Grass both spied a bit of bright stone at the same moment. Bird Girl was quicker and picked it up before Little Grass could get her fingers around it.

"Oh, I want it!" Little Grass cried. "I saw it first!"

Sacagawea wanted it, too. She thought it would be another treasure to add to Quiet Child's medicine bag. But Little Grass looked so unhappy!

"Here it is," said Sacagawea. Little Grass's sad expression changed into a broad smile.

"Can I make a fire with it?" she asked.

"Stones won't make fire by themselves," Sacagawea told her. "But we'll have a new fire when we get down to the river and our tepee is put up again. We'll watch Grandmother make it. Can you make a fire, Willow Girl?"

"I've seen my mother do it, and I know how she does it. But I haven't made one by myself. Can you make it burn?"

"I haven't tried," said Bird Girl, "but I think I know how. You rub the stones and the stick together very hard!"

"And you must have some dry leaves to catch

the sparks and start burning," added Willow Girl. "When we get down to the river I shall ask Mother to let me make the fire."

"Look! Look!" cried Little Grass.

The frame was loaded now and Travels Fast began to ride away, dragging behind him the frame with the tepee loaded on it. Other tepees were being carried away in the same way. Father and the other men had already started on their horses.

Mother came up to get Baby Brother. She examined the cradleboard to see that he was safe and snug. Then she strapped it on her back.

She had another big bundle to carry. Grandmother, too, had a big bundle tied on her back, and another in her arms.

"There is one for you, Bird Girl. Pick it up and come along. Your doll and your new bag are in that bundle."

"Oh, my mother is calling us!" cried Willow Girl. "We have things to carry, too." She and Little Grass hurried away.

Sacagawea picked up her bundle and started off. She felt sure it would feel very heavy before they reached the river.

Then she saw something bright on the ground. It was the stone Little Grass had wanted. After all, she had left it behind. Sacagawea picked it up and tucked it under the strap of her pack. She smiled happily.

"There, Quiet Child," she whispered. "That's another good luck charm to put in your medicine bag."

Travels Fast had gone far ahead of them. He was riding a horse and having such fun!

"Why can't I ride a horse?" Bird Girl asked.

"What a girl!" Grandmother said. "Always asking questions."

But Mother smiled. "Girls must learn to build the house and carry the burdens. That is our share in life. The men are hunters and fighters, but we women look after the home and the food and the babies."

"But why can't we have horses, too?" Sacagawea asked again.

"Well, if there were a great many horses, we could have some, too, after the men and boys have all they need."

"I see," said Bird Girl. But in her heart she was making herself a promise.

"Someday I shall have a horse of my own."

A SWIMMING LESSON

HOW EXCITING IT WAS, down by the river!

Bird Girl laid down her bundle beside the ones which Mother and Grandmother had dropped from their backs, and she ran to the edge of the wide river. She clapped her hands when she saw the fish. There were so many of them that they were pushing and crowding one another as they made their way upstream.

She had never imagined there could be so many fish. As far as she could see, drops of

water splashed in the sun, and sleek fins and tails rose above water and dipped under again.

They were all on their way up the river, toward the land where the sun rose in the morning. The river was going as fast as it could in the other direction, but the big fish swam right on against the current.

"Hooray!" Travels Fast said. "Plenty to eat!"

"Plenty of work," said Grandmother. But she did not say it grumblingly.

Sacagawea thought to herself, "I believe Grandmother likes to work."

Mother explained this. "Plenty of work will mean plenty to eat. No more hungry times just now. Let us hope the men will get a great many more fish than we can eat. Then we can dry some and keep them for the days when there are none left in the river."

"Where do they all go?" asked Sacagawea

curiously. Up and down the stream, she could see the flashing fins.

"That is a big question," said Mother, "and it will take a long time to answer it. Now we have to be busy raising the tepee. But if you ask me tonight, when we have our feast and dance, I'll tell you then."

"A feast and a dance! What fun!" Bird Girl began to prance around, hopping from one foot to the other and pretending that she was beating a drum or tom-tom. The dance, she knew, was just for the men, the hunters and warriors and the medicine men like Old Man. Still, it didn't do any harm to pretend that she was dancing.

"But there is much to do first," Mother reminded her. "You must look after Baby Brother while Grandmother and I set up the tepee, build the fire, and get ready to cook the fish Father and Brother will bring."

Father and Travels Fast had already taken their spears—long rods with sharp stones fastened to the end—and gone to the riverbank, farther downstream. Sacagawea longed to see them spear the fish but knew she must stay.

"Here," Grandmother said, "is a quiet little pool where the water comes in from the river."

Already the younger children were gathering about the pool. Willow Girl and Little Grass dipped their feet in. Little Grass squealed and drew her feet back quickly.

"Cold! Cold!" she called out.

"Don't be afraid," said Willow Girl. "I like it cold. See!" She put her whole foot into the water and held it there for as many counts as all her fingers and toes.

"I like it c-c-cold, too," said Little Grass, trying to do the same thing. But she held her foot in only long enough to count one finger! When she pulled it out again she began to hop around. Even though her skin was used to the outdoors, the water seemed quite cold.

"The water will be warmer soon," said Willow Girl, "when the sun looks over this way. It is coming nearer already."

Mother put Baby Brother's cradleboard against a nearby tree.

"Now, Bird Girl," she said, "you may play in the water if you like, but be sure to look after Baby Brother. Don't let anything knock against him. He will watch you for a while, then fall asleep, in spite of the noise."

Such a lot of noise! More children were coming all the time and they were all laughing and splashing the water. Baby Brother watched from his cradleboard, his brown eyes not missing a thing that went on.

Over in the bushes some of the younger boys

were pretending that they were hunters. They too were having great fun, shouting and laughing. One of them threw a sharp stone up into a tree. But it did not bring down the bird he had aimed at, and the boys ran farther away, pretending to follow the tracks of a rabbit.

Bird Girl's sharp eyes saw, a minute later, that something had fallen from the tree where the boy had aimed his stone. She ran over to see what it was.

It was a magpie, fluttering about helplessly. The stone had injured it, and it could not fly. One of its wings flapped and would not spread out. The bird only fluttered a little when Sacagawea picked it up.

Its feathers were glossy black, with white on its tail. Bird Girl had often watched magpies from a distance, but she had never held one in her hand before. She was smoothing the ruffled

feathers when the boy who had thrown the stone rushed back.

"Here! That's mine!" he shouted, and he snatched the bird from her before she had time to answer. Off he ran. All Sacagawea had left in her hand was one white feather.

"Anyway, I'll keep this for the medicine bag," she thought. "I have a red feather for fire, and now this is a white one for the snow that makes the ground all white!"

Suddenly she heard the girls calling her.

"Oh," she cried, "I am forgetting Baby Brother." She ran back to the tree where the cradleboard was. He was already tired of the noisy bathers. His head was nodding, and he was nearly asleep.

"Look! Look!" shouted Willow Girl. "I am learning to swim!"

Two or three of the older girls were out in the deep water. They were making the drops fly in all directions as they paddled about.

"See! I can do it!" cried Willow Girl.

"I can, too," said Little Grass, stepping now with both feet into the cold water.

"No, you're too little," said her sister. "You stay back there with Bird Girl."

This hurt Sacagawea's feelings. She knew she must stay near her brother, but she did not like to think that she was not old enough to do whatever Willow Girl could do. "Never mind," she said to Little Grass. "We'll show them we can learn to swim here."

"Dog!" cried Little Grass, pointing to a shallow place near by.

One of the little dogs had come down to the pool and was paddling along not far from the edge. He was only a puppy and he was working hard to make his way to a log.

The two girls watched him. They saw his paws moving up and down, up and down.

"I can see how he does it," thought Bird Girl. She walked into the water and began to move her arms and legs the way the dog did. At first she didn't dare take her feet off the sand. By and by she got up enough courage to try it.

"I can swim the way the dog does," she said to Little Grass.

"I can swim, too," laughed Little Grass. But she was not really swimming. She just stood in the shallow water and splashed it with her hands. She was having fun, though. In fact, she and Bird Girl were having so much fun that they forgot about the older girls, who were moving farther and farther away.

"Maybe I'm not a fish yet," Sacagawea said to herself, "but I suppose even the fish have to stay at home until they learn to swim." She wasn't sure she was doing it right, but she did her best to move along as the little dog did. She would go for a few strokes in one direction, paddling hard. Then she would stand up, turn around and paddle back. She wanted to try going into the deeper water, but she knew she must not go too far from her brother in his cradleboard.

Now there was a great shouting. Back again came the boys who a little while before had raced off on their imaginary hunt. With them was a pack of barking dogs. A great chase was on. Sacagawea came to the edge of the water to see what it was all about.

Some furry little creature was running ahead of the boys and dogs. It had dashed out of the bushes and was coming right in her direction.

It was a real hunt they were having, after all!

The little rat or squirrel—she could not tell just what it was—was running almost straight to the pool. After it came the yelping dogs, and behind them the boys, all running and shouting to one another.

Sacagawea got out of the pool and pulled Little Grass up beside her. "We must get Baby Brother out of the way," she said.

The girls had nearly reached Baby Brother when on came the pack of boys and dogs. Then Sacagawea saw one of the big dogs bump into the cradleboard!

She jumped to catch the cradle, but missed it.

The board hit the ground with a thump and the surprised baby cried out.

A still bigger dog came along. Its flying feet hit the cradle and knocked it out of reach!

Then she saw it tumble off into the pool as the great crowd of dogs and boys rushed by!

There was no time to cry out for help. Bird Girl jumped into the water and began to paddle as hard as she could in the direction the cradleboard had gone. In a moment she was in deep water, far over her head! She kept on paddling toward the cradleboard.

The water was whirling around her, but in a few strokes she caught hold of the board. She shook her head to get the water out of her eyes. Then she saw that the board was right side up and that Baby Brother was on top.

But how was she going to get him back to shore? It seemed a long way off. The other girls were too far away to see what had happened. She must try to paddle back to where Little Grass was standing, calling as hard as she could for someone to come.

Sacagawea had to keep one hand tight on the cradleboard to hold it up and push it back to the shore. And with her other hand and her two feet, she tried to paddle her way in to shore. But instead of going toward shore she seemed to go round and round in a circle. Maybe she drew a little nearer the shore as she went around, but she wasn't quite sure. The shore seemed a very long way off.

She did her best to keep moving, but her muscles began to grow tired.

When she was scarcely able to paddle any longer, and her head began to droop, she heard another voice. It was Mother's. "Hold on a moment longer, Bird Girl!"

Then those kind brown hands of Mother's lifted her and Baby Brother out of the water!

"My own good girl!" said Mother.

Sacagawea thought Mother's voice sounded sweeter than any she had ever heard. When she leaned her head against Mother's shoulder, it felt better than any soft fur she had ever had for a pillow.

"The tepee is up now," Mother said. "Better come along and rest a little."

Sacagawea looked around her. There, thrust in the ground at the foot of the tree, was her white feather, just where she had put it for safekeeping. She picked it up and went along with Mother.

Everyone in the camp was happy that evening. The men and boys had had good luck fishing. Already there were rows of fish hanging up to dry. While some of the women had been preparing these fish, others had been preparing a feast. The Shoshone always had feast on the first day of the fishing.

First they had dug a pit and put big stones in the bottom of it. Then they had built a fire on top of the stones and kept it going until the stones were too hot to touch. If a drop of water touched them it sputtered and fizzled like the hiss of a rattlesnake.

Now the big fish were laid on the hot stones and covered with other stones and earth. In the morning they would be dug up again. They would be baked until they almost melted in your mouth, Grandmother had said. The girls could hardly wait to taste them.

Everyone was walking about the camp and chattering and laughing. Even the babies in their cradleboards seemed to chuckle more than usual, and did not want to go to sleep.

"Mother," said Sacagawea, "you promised to tell me where the big fish come from."

"So I did," Mother replied. She was busy, as usual, but her hands could keep on working while she talked.

"You have seen the eggs that crack open for a bird baby to come out?"

Sacagawea nodded.

"Well, fish come from eggs, too," Mother

said. "But they are much smaller and there are many more of them. These big fish came up the river to lay their eggs in places where it is good for the little fish to hatch. So the little fish live far up this stream."

"But where do the big ones come from?" Sacagawea wanted to know.

"Nobody knows exactly, my daughter. All we know is that when they are partly grown the fish swim off down the river. Nobody knows where or how far they go.

"Many moons go by, and the little fish grow big. Then one day they all swim back again, the way you saw them today. They are hurrying back to the places where the river is small."

Sacagawea nodded. "Where does the river go? As far as the sun? It goes the same way."

"It goes much farther than any of the Shoshone have ever been," Mother replied. "Old Man, who often talks about distant countries, has gone down the river to the land where the Chopunnish tribe lives. He has told us many of the things that he learned from them.

"He says that in their country our river joins a much wider one, and the two go on together toward the setting sun. The Chopunnish also say these rivers go on together until they reach a lake so wide that no man can see the end of it. It has a strange smell and is full of salt. The people who live beside it call this lake the stinking water. They do not know how large it is or where it ends."

"I would like to see it," said Sacagawea. "Mother, will we ever go down to the end of the river? I would like to do that."

"We shall never go that far," Grandmother said. "There are too many enemy tribes on the way. You are not a fish, to swim downstream."

Bird Girl did not answer, but she thought, "If I can swim in a little pool today, maybe a day will come when I can swim in big rivers. And I would come back, too, like the big fish."

She said the last part aloud, but she was so sleepy that Grandmother did not catch her words. "Put a robe over the child," Grandmother said to Mother. "She has fallen asleep."

Mother tucked her up carefully. "She has had a tiring day, our Bird Girl. She is a busy child."

"She thinks of Baby Brother first," Grandmother added. "She was a brave one today. Not many young girls would have done that."

"She is quick to act, and thinks of others instead of herself. She will be a good mother when she grows up."

Sacagawea did not hear. She was asleep now, with her hand on the bag in which she had laid the white feather carefully beside the red one. Already she was dreaming. In her dream she was a shining fish. She was swimming down the swift stream, past the lands of the Chopunnish, to the lake which people called the stinking water.

LEARNING ABOUT
THE SETTLERS

FATHER AND MOST OF the men had gone to get horses. They had been away a long time, and the women were anxiously waiting for them to come back.

Many moons had gone by since Sacagawea had first learned to swim. Three more times they had gone down to the river to spear fish, and three times they had come back to their camping place in the high mountains.

Three times they had gone far in the other direction, toward the rising sun, to hunt the buffalo. No one had to carry Baby Brother any longer. He was out of his cradleboard long ago, and was called Little Brother or Younger Brother now.

At first he kept close beside Bird Girl, but now he played with the other boys and came back to the tepee only when he was hungry or very tired.

As for Travels Fast, he was almost a man now. He was a real hunter and brought much game back to the tepee.

"Someday," he told his sister, "I'll have a fight with a Crow or a Chopunnish. Then I'll come back with a scalp lock of hair from the head of an enemy, and I'll be a real warrior."

"After they have a medicine dance," Sacagawea reminded him. She had seen older boys being announced as grown fighters, and knew that they had to take part in a ceremony to prove their courage.

"Yes, that's right," Travels Fast said, "and maybe you'll be old enough then to carry around some food for us men." Sacagawea knew that he was teasing her, but she let him think that she didn't mind.

When she was old enough for that, she would probably be called Bird Woman instead of Bird Girl. But when he was a real warrior, Travels Fast would probably take an entirely new name. This new name would tell of some brave deed, or something he had done. All the young men changed their names in this way.

She was thinking about this when Younger Brother hurried up, his round brown face shining with excitement.

"Old Man says they are coming!" he cried.

"Who's coming?" Of course she guessed what he meant, but she wanted to hear him say it.

"All the men!" shouted the boy. "And lots of horses! I was up on the hillside with Old Man. He saw them, far off." Younger Brother pointed to the south.

The news brought all the people out of their tepees. They gathered together to watch. First they could see figures moving. Then they began to hear the sounds of the running horses.

Sacagawea was in front of the crowd. She was glad to see Father coming, on a strong-looking brown horse.

When the warriors rode in, all the camp broke into shouts of greeting and praise.

"I'm going to ride one of those horses," Sacagawea said to herself. But now Travels Fast and the boys of his group were taking them off to the corral. They would ride them often, she knew. But she would wait for a chance. Some day, she was sure, a chance would come.

Besides the horses, the men had brought back two guns! Father had one of them.

This was a real treasure. The Shoshone had only a few of these "shooting sticks." They guarded them very carefully.

"You may look it over well," Father said to Travels Fast, "but then I shall have to give it to Old Man. He takes care of all these shooting sticks when we are not using them."

Travels Fast handled it with great care. He patted the long smooth barrel. He held the gun

up to his shoulder and pretended to shoot a bird
on the limb of a far-off tree.

"Bang! Bang!" cried Younger Brother, who
was watching him.

"Silly!" said Bird Girl. "There's nothing in it
to go *bang*."

"There will be," Father told her. "Your
brother does well with his bow and arrow. Now
he shall learn to use this, too."

"Me too!" said Younger Brother. He was

hopping up and down with excitement and trying to take the gun into his own hands. But Travels Fast would let him put his hand only on the long round part.

"Where did it come from?" he asked.

"A *tabba bone* made it," Father said. Everyone looked at him and then at the shooting stick.

"Tabba bone" meant a man with a pale face, a white man. The Shoshone had long ago heard about these people from far-off lands. But none of the tribe had ever seen one.

"Did you see a *tabba bone*?" asked Travels Fast. His voice was low and serious.

"Not exactly," Father said. "We did not go far enough away for that. But the people we did see, down in the country of the Utes, have visited the *tabba bone.* They told us a great deal about them. You know the *tabba bone* are far, far down there." He pointed to the south.

"Aren't they in that direction, too?" Travels Fast pointed toward the morning sun.

"Yes, there, too. Before these *tabba bone* came, our people had never seen any horses or guns. They did not even know that such things were in the world. Then one day the *tabba bone* came riding across the land on their great four-legged beasts. They were wearing something that shone in the sun and clanked as they rode. In their hands they carried shooting sticks such as this one and long sharp knives and axes.

"When our people saw these strange beings they thought the men and horses were single animals, with many arms and legs."

"Were our people afraid?" asked Little Brother. "I think I would have been."

"Many of them were," Father replied. "They had a right to be afraid, too. They had no weapons as deadly as the white man's shooting stick. Their axes were not as sharp as the white man's axes, and their knives were not so long.

"I have heard that still farther to the south the white men make the tribes there dig deep under the ground, where they cannot see the sun all day. They find the stuff they use to make their knives. They put it in the fire to make it hard and do other things to it, too. They know many things, these men of the white faces.

"Stay awake tonight, my son, and listen at the victory dance. You will hear a fine story."

Before night came, Sacagawea slipped quietly from the tepee to the corral where the horses were kept. Most of the women and girls were making ready for the feast, and the men were resting from their trip.

She crept around to the side of the cotton-wood fence that was farthest from the tepees.

The palings were sharp when she climbed on top of them, but she managed to balance herself where it did not hurt too much.

Some of the horses were eating dried grass the boys had thrown in for them. Others were moving around the corral. But none of them came close enough for her to see or touch.

"If I climb down inside," she told herself, "I shall not be tall enough to get on the back of one of them."

Then a thought came to her. "I'll go get some grass for them."

Soon she was back with an armful of grass, and up again on the fence. None of the horses noticed her at first. By and by some of them seemed to smell the grass and came over to where she was perched on the fence.

She kept very quiet so that she would not frighten them away. After a while a graceful young horse came still closer and began to eat her bunch of grass. He was light brown and had a white star-shaped spot on his head.

"That is a star on his forehead," thought Sacagawea. "I do believe this is one of the horses Father brought this morning! I shall pretend he is mine. I shall call him Star."

So she slipped off the fence onto the back of the horse.

Star was frightened to feel this sudden weight on his back. He threw up his hooves and ran.

Bird Girl thought she was going to tumble off, but she took hold of Star's mane and held on. Star ran and ran, around and around the corral. Gradually his pace became slower.

"Why, I can ride!" Bird Girl said. But no one heard her except the horses.

Once Star ran close to another horse and she was nearly brushed off. Then he kicked up his hooves a little and she went sliding forward against his neck.

Soon Bird Girl began to tire of her rough ride. How could she get off without falling and perhaps being trampled by the other horses? She had seen Brother pull a strip that ran from the horses mouth, but she did not have anything to pull but the long hair of the mane. So she pulled that, and Star kicked a little higher.

Again she almost fell off. But they were getting near the fence, and an idea came to her. She would try to get him near the fence, and then see if she could jump off or catch hold of the fence.

She pulled at the horse's mane, and several long yellow hairs came off in her hand. Star shuddered a little but kept on running.

He was coming closer to the fence, however, and at last was running close to it. Sacagawea took a long breath, grabbed one of the fence posts as she let go of the mane, and found herself clinging to the pole while Star ran on without her.

She scrambled over the fence and down on the outside. After resting for a while, she started toward the tepee, limping a little. She felt sore where she had rubbed against the horses and against the fence, and her arms ached from holding onto Star's mane. Maybe it wasn't so easy to ride a horse after all.

"But I have started to learn, anyway," she told herself happily.

In her hand she had several long brownish-yellow horsehairs.

"I shall braid these into a charm for Quiet Child's medicine bag," she thought.

Little Brother was too sleepy to hear the story at the dance. Soon his brown eyes closed and he let his head drop down on Grandmother's knee.

Bird Girl promised herself she would stay awake no matter how tired and sleepy she felt. She wanted to hear more about the men with the white faces.

She had heard people talk about them before. But she had thought they were like the coyotes that talked and the bears that turned to men in the stories which Grandmother often told.

These things might have happened long ago, but there was no use expecting them to happen again for her to see.

Now from what Father had said, she thought the pale-faced ones must be real men like the Shoshone, only different in appearance. She wanted to hear everything she could about them. So she listened very intently to what the singing and dancing men had to say.

In the big council tepee the women kept feeding the fire while the men danced. The leaping flames and the leaping figures made strange shadows across the ground and upon the circle of older women and children who sat watching.

"They came! The men of white faces came!" one of the dancers was chanting as he leaped forward and back, in the firelight.

Another took up the song: "Across the great water they came!"

From across the fire came a voice: "On two feet they walked! On four feet, they rode!"

"Oh-h-h!" A little chorus went around the line of listeners.

"Fast were their horses!"

"Faster still flew the balls from their shooting sticks! They followed the eagle and he fell to the ground! They followed the deer and the deer ran no more! They followed the fleeing men and the men fell and rose no more!"

"Ah-h-h!" It was a wail of sorrow that came from the listeners this time.

The dancers' voices grew happier.

"Now we have horses and can ride like the wind!"

"Now we have shooting sticks, and the deer fall before us!"

"Now our enemies tremble before us! They too will fall!"

"Oh-h-h." It was a fierce cry this time, from both dancers and listeners.

Sacagawea shivered a little. "Is this a war dance?" she asked.

Mother smiled. "No. They are remembering other times. They are happy over the guns and horses they have brought back."

"Now we have guns and horses like the men of pale faces! We are men! We are warriors! None shall escape us!" chanted the dancing men.

"Are we really as strong as they are?" Bird Girl asked.

"We know how to use the shooting sticks," Grandmother answered. "But when they grow old and do not work we have to go back and try to get others. Old Man says the *tabba bone* know how to make them and mend them, too."

"Has Old Man seen these men?"

"No, none of the Shoshone has ever seen them.

But the man who first brought us horses was the son of a *tabba bone* and an Indian woman. That white-faced father lived for many moons in the camp of his wife's people."

Sacagawea listened with excitement. "Someday I shall see a *tabba bone,* too," she said to herself. When she went to sleep that night, she dreamed that a whole village of people with pale faces were dancing about her.

The Shoshone think much about their dreams, but Bird Girl did not tell hers to anyone except Willow Girl. The two talked about it the next morning, whispering so that Little Grass would not hear them and tell.

A BASKET AND A DRESS

"OUR BIRD GIRL is growing taller," said Grandmother. "Now that she can ride a horse—"

She smiled at Sacagawea, who looked down at the ground and said nothing. Sacagawea did not know that Grandmother knew of her trips to the corral. She had grown quite friendly with Star, and almost never fell off his back now.

Grandmother laughed. "Yes, nearly big enough to—"

"To what?" asked Sacagawea. She hoped

Grandmother meant she could have a horse to ride, but Grandmother was thinking of something else.

"First, to make a neat basket, and then to make yourself a fine robe of skin."

"Let me begin now," said Bird Girl. Willow Girl was already at work on her first big basket and was feeling very important about it.

"Come with me," said Grandmother. "We'll get some small branches from the willows down by the stream."

How they searched down by the stream! They must have branches of the same thickness and long enough to go down one side of the basket and come up on the other side. They would cross one another at the bottom of the basket.

"You can't bend them to the shape of the basket now," warned Grandmother. Sacagawea tried just the same.

Snap! went one of the straightest branches.

"You see?" said Grandmother. "They will have to be soaked in water a long time before they can be bent without breaking."

Bird Girl hunted and hunted before she found another branch as good as the one she had broken. She wandered off up the stream and stopped to listen to a blue jay chattering about something that must have gone wrong in his world. Sacagawea wished, as she had wished many times, that she could understand bird talk.

But when Mr. Blue Jay stopped scolding and fluttered away, he left something behind. As Sacagawea's bright eyes spied it, her hand went out and caught it before the breeze could carry it off. It was a beautiful blue tail feather. "Another one for the medicine bag," she said to herself. With a strip of reed she tied the feather to the branches she was gathering.

Grandmother smiled when she saw this, but she said nothing. She always knew things, it seemed, the way she knew about the horses. But she did not talk about them until she was ready.

When they got back to the camp, Sacagawea slipped into the tepee to put the blue feather away with Quiet Child's other treasures.

"I'm not going to have so much time to be with you," she told Quiet Child, "now that I have to make a big basket, and then a dress. But I'll keep looking, and maybe I'll find other things for you." Quiet Child did not speak, but she looked almost as wise as Grandmother.

Sacagawea and Grandmother made many trips to gather branches and twigs and grasses for the basket. It was a great pile when they brought it all together, but Sacagawea knew that it would be much smaller when she had woven it.

First the grasses and reeds were dyed. Some were to be left their natural color, so they were soaked in clear water. Others were to be black, so they were soaked in water darkened with charcoal from the fire. The bark of the willow tree made yellow to dye others. And the juice of the pokeberry made a lovely red color. "I always thought that pokeberries ought to be of some use," said Bird Girl. "They are so pretty."

"Useful things are always good to look at," said Grandmother.

Sacagawea hoped the basket would be good to look at as well as to use.

Summer was nearly over before she actually began the weaving. First she crisscrossed the long willow sticks and bent them into the shape she wanted. Then she tied them together with stout grass. She would take the grass off later, when the weaving began to hold the sticks in place.

She had decided that the pattern on the basket would be the sun coming up over a mountain top. She remembered the day she ran away to see the sun begin its journey in the morning, and couldn't find the way back until Brother found her sleeping. She still wondered how far away the sun was. Since that time they had gone many sleeps to the east to hunt the buffalo, but each time the sun seemed just as far away as ever.

There was a great deal to learn about making a basket. Sometimes her hands grew tired. Sometimes bending over the work for a long time made her back stiff. But it was fun to see the basket grow and to weave the colors so that the pattern began to show more clearly.

"Perhaps," she thought to herself, "I can find time to make a small basket for Quiet Child."

Grandmother was making a basket, too, side by side with Sacagawea. Bird Girl watched and learned with her eyes while she listened and learned with her ears.

"It will be a good basket, I think," Grandmother said one day. This made Bird Girl happy. Grandmother did not often say words of praise.

She wondered if it would be as pretty as Willow Girl's basket, but she did not like to ask.

"If you are a very good basketmaker," Grandmother told her, "Father will be much pleased. The warrior who comes to buy you for his wife will have to pay many horses for you."

Mother smiled. "Maybe enough so that I can have a horse to ride when we travel."

"And one for me?" asked Sacagawea.

"No," Grandmother answered. "You won't be here with all those fine horses. You will be with your husband. And he won't have so many horses, because he has paid them to get you."

This didn't seem exactly fair to Bird Girl. "If I am worth so many horses, it seems to me I should have one for myself."

"You must wait until you, too, have a little girl who grows up to be a good basketmaker. Then someone will give a lot of horses for her."

"Oh, dear," said Sacagawea. "That sounds too far away. It might almost be forever."

The days passed, and each day Sacagawea worked hard on her basket. At last she tied the last reeds in place. "There," she said. "My basket is finished. See the sun shining on this side?"

Willow Girl looked at the picture of the sun which Sacagawea had woven into the basket. "My basket has a star on each side," she said.

"I like the sun," Bird Girl said. "It makes all the hills so bright."

"But the stars shine when the world would be

all black without them," said Willow Girl.

"When I start my basket," said Little Grass, "I shall put the moon on it!" Sacagawea and Willow Girl smiled at each other. They knew it would be many moons before Little Grass would start her basket.

"Now, I suppose, I shall begin work on my dress," said Bird Girl. "It's hard work, isn't it?"

"Indeed it *is* hard," said Willow Girl. "I pound and pound and scrape and scrape at that deerskin until my arms ache. I don't know whether I'll *ever* get the skin soft enough and smooth enough. I don't see how the deer could wear it when it was so hard and rough." She drew a long breath. "I get so tired of it! Sometimes I don't care whether I ever have a dress or not!"

"Older girls have to have dresses, Grandmother says, even if it is hard work. After all, it will be fun wearing them when they are finished."

"I guess it will," Willow Girl admitted, "but it *is* a lot of trouble. When will you start working on yours?"

"Grandmother says we shall begin as soon as we find a deer or an antelope in front of our tepee. I suppose that means the next time Father comes home."

But it was not Father who brought the deer for Sacagawea's dress. One day Travels Fast came home from a hunt with the other boys. "Look here!" he shouted happily and threw down before Mother and Grandmother the deer he had been half carrying and half dragging.

They were all proud of him. Little Brother danced around the deer and clapped his hands.

"Almost a warrior," Grandmother said, approvingly.

Mother looked at her tall young son as if she wished he could stay like Little Brother, but she smiled, even though she looked a little sad. "My hunter son," she said.

"This will make you a fine dress," Grandmother told Bird Girl. "We shall stake the skin out here to dry."

Sacagawea hurried to tell Willow Girl about it. "Brother is almost a grown man now. Soon he will be a real warrior."

"He will have to be in the Sun Dance, then," said Willow Girl.

"Oh!" Bird Girl had not thought of that. Of course he would have to show everyone that he was brave enough to be a warrior. She had seen the young men dangling against the poles in the Sun Dance. She hoped staying there staring at the sun would not hurt Elder Brother too much.

"We must both hurry with our dresses," said Willow Girl. "I want to have mine finished before the next victory dance."

"Mine will take longer," Sacagawea. "But maybe I can finish it before Elder Brother is a warrior."

Sacagawea was scraping away at the deerskin one day when Willow Girl came across the space that separated their tepee homes.

"My dress is nearly ready to sew," Willow Girl told her.

"I wish mine were!" sighed Bird Girl. She was not sorry to stop for a while and brush her long black hair away from her face. "It will be a long time yet before I can sew."

"Long ago I made a dress for my doll," said Willow Girl. "But that wasn't like this dress making. Mother gave me a piece of buckskin all ready to use. I poked a hole in it for her head and smaller holes to put her arms through. She is made of skin, too, but it is darker than the dress. Then I tied a strip around her waist and I thought she was all dressed up."

"She looked nice, anyway." Sacagawea remembered how she had admired Willow Girl's doll. "But you haven't brought her out to play with for a long time."

"Mother says I am too big for doll now, and I'd better give her to Little Grass. Maybe I will, after my dress is ready to wear."

"I don't have time to play with my doll anymore," said Sacagawea. "She just leans against the side of the tepee all day long. But I like to talk to her a little bit before I go to sleep."

"You'll have to put her away pretty soon," said Willow Girl. Her friend seemed very grown-up about everything, Sacagawea thought.

That afternoon Sacagawea went quietly into the tepee when no one was near. Mother was making moccasins and Grandmother had gone for wood. She went over to Quiet Child and the medicine bag that always lay beside her.

She opened the medicine bag and laid out the treasures. There were several bright stones, two or three odd-shaped bones, three pretty shells, and a little piece of buckskin. Quiet Child wore the buckskin as a cap when she was playing at being a medicine woman, directing a dance around the fire.

Last of all, Bird Girl smoothed out the three feathers. There was the red one for fire, the white snow feather, and the blue feather, the color of the sky overhead.

"Red, white, and blue!" exclaimed Bird Girl. "How pretty they look!"

Then she carefully put them all back in the bag again. "I don't know when we'll have time for another play dance," she told Quiet Child. "Maybe when I get this dress finished."

Moons came and went before it was finished. It was a great day when Sacagawea began the sewing. With Grandmother's sharp-pointed knife she made slits through which she drew the long thin leather strips that held the pieces together. It reminded her of the bag she had made for Quiet Child long before.

Then there was the fringe to hang around the bottom of the dress and on the sleeves. It was fun cutting this, but she had to do it very carefully.

She had gathered some shells at the river the last time the salmon came, and these were fastened at the front. Sacagawea thought they looked very bright and pretty.

Altogether it was a dress which the other girls would admire. Both Mother and Grandmother were pleased with it. They were pleased, too, with the steady way Sacagawea had kept working, day after day.

They merely smiled one day when they saw Sacagawea slipping away among the trees with Quiet Child and the medicine bag.

"This may be our last playtime," she told Quiet Child, as again she laid out the treasures and made Quiet Child into a medicine woman. "I suppose Mother will take you and keep you for her first granddaughter. But you'll be my dolly just the same, won't you?" She hugged Quiet Child to her and felt a lump in her throat. It was like losing a friend, she thought.

Willow Girl was waiting for her when she came back. "My dress is finished and put away," Willow Girl said. "Yours must be nearly finished by now, too."

"It is," said Sacagawea. "We can wear them at the same dance, Mother says."

"Let's practice plaiting our hair now," said Willow Girl. "I'll do yours first. My mother says after our dance I will be called Willow Woman instead of Willow Girl. And you will be called Bird Woman. But I really think my mother will keep on calling me Girl."

"I'm sure mine will, too," said Sacagawea.

THE SUN DANCE

LITTLE GRASS CAME RUNNING excitedly to Sacagawea. "I just saw your Elder Brother going into the medicine tepee. A lot of the big boys went in. Hear what a noise they are making! But I can't tell what it is all about."

"I know," Bird Girl told her. "Old Man and some of the others are listening while the boys tell what they have done. They're telling about all the horses they have taken and the enemies they've killed and—oh, just everything. Then the old men will decide whether they are ready to be chosen for the Sun Dance. After the dance, if they're chosen, they will become warriors."

A still louder noise arose from the medicine tepee. "But why do they shout so loudly?" Sacagawea went on.

"Mother told me about that," said Willow Girl. "The boys act their hunts all over again for the men to see. But some of them claim more than they did. Then the others tell their stories and the men have to decide which is right."

"Is your brother going to be a warrior?" Little Grass asked Sacagawea.

"I think so," answered Bird Girl. "That's what he went in for. He has a lot of things to tell about and a scalp lock to put on the end of his spear. My dress is made from skins he brought to us."

She and Willow Girl felt very proud and grown-up now that they were wearing their new dresses. Sometimes Little Grass seemed too young to talk to at all. But answering her questions made them feel important.

When she was not around they practiced calling each other Willow Woman and Bird Woman. The new names sounded so odd they giggled over them a good deal.

"This is the third day inside the medicine tepee," said Willow Girl. "Tomorrow they will put up the lodge for the dance. We can all go in and see it."

"Will they make a tepee as big as that?" Little Grass waved her arm toward the circle of tepees that formed the camp.

"It's not exactly a tepee," said Sacagawea. "It hasn't any top. The sun shines right down into it. First they'll put up a tall, tall pole in the center. The boys are strapped against it by strips of leather under their skin. They have to look right at the sun. After a while their skin breaks and they fall to the ground."

"Oh! Do you mean they're tied up by their own skin? Doesn't it hurt?"

"Of course it hurts," said Willow Girl. "But they hang there with the sun in their eyes and don't complain. That's the way they show they are brave enough to be warriors."

This raised a question in Sacagawea's mind. She went to Grandmother and Mother for her answer. They were working together not far away. When Willow Girl had gone off, with Little Grass beside her, Bird Girl came up to them.

"Don't girls have to be brave, too?" she asked.

"They don't fight our enemies," Grandmother answered.

"But is killing things the only way to be brave?"

"Not at all," said Mother. "You will need courage for many things, even though you are not a warrior."

"Indeed," said Grandmother, "I once heard of quite a little girl who hadn't learned to swim. But when her baby brother tumbled into the water she went right after him, into the deep water. Don't you think that was brave?"

They both smiled at Bird Girl. She looked down at the ground and didn't say anything.

But it gave her a very happy feeling inside to

think that they remembered that day, long ago.

"I shall try always to be brave," she thought to herself.

All the next day, as Sacagawea worked with Grandmother, she could see the building of the medicine lodge. First a tall tree was placed in the center and all but a few top branches were stripped off. Then the ground around it was carefully smoothed for the dancers. Next a place was made for the fire, and finally a circle of smaller poles was put up around the tall one. All the women and children and others who could not take part in the dance would gather outside these poles to watch.

Before the sun set, the lodge was all ready for the dance the next day. The Shoshone gathered about the entrance, and Old Man came out and stood before them.

Sacagawea, with Little Brother beside her,

was up in the front to hear the names of the warriors who could be tested in the morning.

Travels Fast's name was the very first one called out. How happy they felt! Little Brother hopped up and down for joy.

Everyone else in the camp was saying, "Ah-h-h," as if they thought the judges had made a good choice.

"Does Brother dance?" Little Brother asked.

"No, the men who are already warriors dance. Brother and the other young men must show their courage by cutting a place on their chests for the leather strip to run through."

"This way?" asked Little Brother of Grandmother, who was just behind them. He reached for the knife she always wore at her belt.

"Don't you try it, child. This knife is for cutting wood. Cutting your flesh requires a special knife. And the older men must say some special words over it, or it won't do any good.

"This knife of mine," Grandmother went on, "must go with me now, late as it is, to get some wood. We can't let our fires go out just because there is a fire in the medicine lodge."

"May I go with you?" asked Sacagawea.

"Borrow your mother's wood knife and come along. You will have a knife of your own very soon now."

They had to go a long way, for all the smaller wood near the camp had been gathered. They could still see the sun, but it would not be long before it disappeared.

"I am glad to have you with me, child," said Grandmother. "I do not see so well as I did when I was younger."

When they had gathered two big bundles of wood, all they could carry, they turned back toward the valley. From that distance they could see now and then the flicker of campfires. But they were much higher up the hillside than the camp was.

They were walking on a steep rocky slope when Bird Girl happened to look up and see a big stone teetering on a ledge above them. "Look out, Grandmother!" she called quickly. "Hurry!" They both scrambled out of the way as the stone came crashing down through the bushes.

In her hurry Grandmother tripped and fell.

Bird Girl rushed over to her. Grandmother was lying quite still. "Grandmother, are you all right?" Bird Girl cried.

For a moment Grandmother could not speak. Then in a faint voice she said, "I can't get up just yet, my granddaughter."

At that moment Sacagawea's keen ears heard a sound. She knew instantly what it meant. It was a snake rustling through the fallen leaves.

She looked about her quickly. There it was! It was a big rattlesnake, angry because the falling stone had overturned the log beside which he had been sleeping.

Now he was coiling up, and his dark shiny eyes were looking straight at Grandmother. In a moment he would be ready to strike.

Grandmother saw the snake, too, but she was unable to move. Sacagawea had not a second to lose. She stooped quickly but quietly and picked up a stone. As she rose she let it fly at the snake's ugly head.

Her aim was good. The head fell and the rattling stopped. Then the girl snatched Mother's knife from her belt and struck at the rattler's head. A few blows made her sure that the snake would never hurt anyone.

"You have saved my life," said Grandmother. "And now," she added, "you are going to have a hard time to help me get home. I think I have broken my ankle, and my back is hurt, too. We shall have to leave the wood where we dropped it when the big stone fell."

"I can come back for it," said Sacagawea.

Grandmother was thin and little, as old Shoshone women usually were. Still, it was not easy to hold her up and help her hobble on her one good foot all the way home.

At last they were there. Mother helped make Grandmother more comfortable on some buffalo robes near the fire. "We can't get the man who fixes broken bones for another day," Grandmother said. "He will be too busy with the Sun Dance."

"Now I must go back for our wood," said Sacagawea when Grandmother was settled.

"But it is nearly dark."

"I know the way, and I can hurry."

"You are a brave girl, Sacagawea," said her grandmother. "You don't need a Sun Dance to prove that."

As Sacagawea went off, she was thinking about this. "Surely Grandmother is bravest of all. The pain made great drops of sweat stand out on her forehead, but she didn't make a sound. Surely that takes as much courage as fighting."

Next morning began the big day of the Sun Dance. Willow Girl and Little Grass were starting toward the dance lodge when they met Sacagawea hurrying in the opposite direction.

"Come with us," begged Little Grass.

"Little Grass won't remember a thing about it," said Willow Girl.

"I will, too," said Little Grass.

"But she thinks she has to see everything."

"That's the way with Little Brother," Sacagawea said. "He's already there. But I still have the other bundle of wood to get. I couldn't carry them both last night."

"How is your grandmother this morning?" asked Willow Girl. She had heard about the big rock and the snake the night before.

"She can't get up yet," said Bird Girl. "Mother is worried about her. Save a place for me, will you? I'll hurry back as fast as I can."

The two sisters watched the old men bring the peace pipe and the white bones of the buffalo head into the lodge and put them in the place of honor. Almost before the chanting of the words that called upon the sun to look down on them, Bird Girl was hurrying into the lodge and sitting down beside her friends.

"You haven't missed very much," Willow Girl told her. "The dancers will soon be coming in."

"Is that the same pipe as last year?" asked Bird Girl.

"Oh, yes. Old Man keeps it in his leather trunk. He takes good care of the pipe and the skull. Something terrible would happen to us all if he should lose them."

"I ought to get a pipe for Quiet Child's bag," Sacagawea said to herself and then stopped suddenly in her thoughts. Mother had said Quiet Child and her belongings must be put away now and had put them in the leather trunk in the tepee. Now when Sacagawea put out her hand at night she did not find Quiet Child sitting beside her sleeping place.

Maybe she wouldn't see her dolly again until she saw some younger girl playing with it. Would that other girl also make medicine with the bright stones and the feathers of red and white and blue? She was thinking about this when Little Grass suddenly gave a cry of astonishment.

The dancers were coming in, decorated with

bright paint and wearing feathers in their hair. How they pranced up and down! Some of them the girls recognized. Others were so changed by the strange spots and streaks of paint on their faces that the girls could scarcely guess who they were.

After them came the four old medicine men. Old Man himself was leading. They went to the north, east, south, and west, scattered some sand on the ground, and blew some feather-down into the air. All the while they were chanting a song to the sun. They were asking it to bless them and to give courage and strength to the young men who were on trial.

Then came the young men themselves, Travels Fast leading the group. It was not very pleasant to watch them making gashes in their skin so that the leather thongs might slip through, but they must show how brave they could be. Sacagawea kept her eyes on Travels Fast. She was proud to see that he did not flinch, even when he was tied close to the sun pole and stood there almost dangling, on tiptoe.

The dancing grew faster and wilder now. Sacagawea could see that Elder Brother was in pain, but he was not making any sign or outcry. She thought of Grandmother, whose back hurt her so badly that she could not move without a sharp pain. Yet she, too, was silent and did not cry out. Surely Grandmother was as brave as any of the warriors.

In another day the Sun Dance would be over and Travels Fast would be praised as a brave man and a warrior. His wounds would soon heal. But what would happen to Grandmother's injured back, and to her ankle? Sacagawea did not know.

After the Sun Dance was over, the medicine man would come and push her bones into place and say some charms, or chant a song. Maybe that would help her walk again.

"It takes the longest while to learn all those things they are chanting," Willow Girl was saying. "They have to practice over and over, in the secret tepee, before they get them right."

"If I knew one of the healing songs," said Sacagawea, "I'd go right now and sing it for Grandmother."

TO THE PLAINS
FOR BUFFALO

TWICE SINCE THE Sun Dance the moon had grown into a big round ball in the sky. Twice it had grown smaller night by night until it had disappeared entirely.

Now, all over the Shoshone camp, the people began to say to one another: "It must be nearly time to go down on the plains and hunt the buffalo."

Grandmother was now able to get up from

her bed of skins. But she could not stand so straight as she once did. She had to lean heavily on a thick stick. She was still very busy, but mostly at work that kept her near the tepee.

No one spoke about it, but Sacagawea could see that Mother was worried. Grandmother grew thinner, and her voice was not so strong.

Now at last they were building fires on high places to tell the hunters it was time to come in and get ready for the great buffalo hunt. They must go in a large party, for their enemies would be down on the plains hunting the buffalo, too.

Finally they were all gathered together. At night the men danced and chanted their songs, hoping for a successful hunt and for triumph over their enemies.

In the morning the camp was very busy. The women were taking down the tepee poles. Soon they would be ready to move.

Sacagawea helped Mother take down their tepee. Grandmother tried hard, but she was no longer strong enough to handle it.

"Daughter," she said at last, "I cannot go with you to follow the buffalo."

"Oh, no!" Mother gave a little sharp cry, as if something had suddenly hurt her.

"Do not grieve, daughter. It will not be long."

Sacagawea listened with a heavy heart. What would the journey be like without Grandmother? All her years—about twelve now—Grandmother had been her adviser and her guide. Grandmother's wisdom and experience had told her what to do when any emergency occurred.

"Do not worry, my child," Grandmother said. "You will help make me a shelter and a fire down by the stream."

So while the rest of the packing was finished,

Sacagawea and Grandmother made a small brush shelter near the edge of the stream. Little Grass helped to gather wood for Grandmother's fire. Even Little Brother brought some sticks, though usually he was very scornful of anything he called "girl's work."

He was not very big yet—not so tall as Little Grass—but he was very proud to think he was not a girl like her. He could play with the dogs and even sometimes beg a ride on one of the horses. But Little Grass had to stay with the women and learn to do other things.

The children had gathered a large pile of wood before the poles of the home tepee were tied up and ready to be hauled away.

"I wish there were more food to leave for you," said Mother. It had been a hungry time and there was not much left. But Little Brother had snared a squirrel the day before, and Mother still had a few pieces of hard biscuit made by pounding together sunflower seed and wild cherries, pits and all.

"I shall do very well," Grandmother told them. "Do not worry about me."

As the last Shoshone moved off to the east, Bird Girl looked back to see Grandmother sitting on the bank of the stream, watching them.

For several hours the tribe moved slowly but steadily toward the land where the sun comes up. The men rode ahead, scouting the way, while the women and children followed on foot. Sacagawea, Willow Girl, and Little Grass walked along together.

At last they came to a high hill and started to climb it. Sacagawea fell behind the others.

"We go up for a long, long time," Willow Girl told Little Grass. "But we go down even longer."

"When do we reach the big river?"

"Oh, that will be a long time—more sleeps than my fingers."

"I wish we'd find a buffalo right now," said Little Grass. "I'm hungry."

"We're all hungry," said her sister, "but the buffalo are far, far away. You just keep your eyes open. Maybe you can see some roots to dig, or some berries to pick."

Sure enough, Little Grass's bright eyes soon spied on the hillside some plants whose roots, she knew, were good to eat. Both girls started digging away.

But when Sacagawea came up, she looked farther ahead and saw a bush with bright berries. How good they looked! How much better they tasted to the hungry girls! Mother came along and laid down her bundle to help pick them. There was quite a pile.

"Mother," said Sacagawea, "may I carry a basket of berries back to Grandmother?"

"It is a long way," said Mother.

"I know the way and I will hurry fast," said Bird Girl. "Do let me, Mother."

"All right," said Mother, "but you will have to fly like a bird."

"Take some of my roots," said Little Grass, bringing up a big handful.

"That is good of you," said Sacagawea, putting her arms about the younger girl. "Grandmother will be glad you thought of her."

Back Sacagawea hurried by the way she had come, first passing some of the later travelers and then making her way alone down the hill and through the trees. The way seemed longer when she was alone.

At last she came in sight of the deserted place where the Shoshone camp had been. Grandmother was huddled in front of her little shelter, her arms folded across her knees and her head resting on her arms. She looked up in surprise when Bird Girl called to her.

"I did not think I would see you again," she said, when Sacagawea had given her the roots and the berries. "It is good of you young people to think of me.

"And now," she went on, "you must be

hurrying back. The stars will be out before you reach the camp, and everyone will be settling down for the sleeping time.

"I think there are friendly stars up there, who send the light down to show your way. When you see them, remember they will be looking down on me, too, and I shall be wishing you a safe journey."

Sacagawea knelt down and laid her head on Grandmother's shoulder. "I wish you could come with me," she said.

"My heart will always be with you," Grandmother told her. "I think the stars will tell you that when you look up at them. Good-bye, my child."

Sacagawea hurried away, looking back from time to time until Grandmother was hidden behind a hill. Then she followed on after the others, heavy-hearted and close to tears.

It was dark by the time she came to the camp and found her parents' tepee. After one look at her face, Mother fed her and put her to bed.

Next morning the tepees were taken down and the band moved on. On and on they traveled, up hill and down. Sometimes trees and rough bushes brushed against the girls' faces as they went along. Sometimes they hobbled over fields of prickly pear. These were small plants whose spines almost cut through their moccasins.

Now and then they came across traces of the journeys which the Shoshone had made in other years. But even with these signs to help them, the trail was difficult to follow.

Willow Girl and Sacagawea knew from other journeys how long this one would be. But Little Grass got up every morning thinking this day she would surely see the buffalo. All day long she watched for them. At night she would say, "Well, maybe we shall find them tomorrow."

Some of the men hunted every day for antelope or deer or smaller animals so there would be food. But there never seemed to be enough for all the hungry travelers. So the girls kept their eyes open for anything that could be eaten.

"I believe I could eat a whole buffalo myself," said Little Grass one day.

The older girls laughed. "You don't remember how big they are. It would take you all day to eat just part of one."

"Will we have plenty to eat when we get to them?" asked Little Grass.

"Oh, yes," said Willow Girl, "plenty to eat right away, and plenty more to hang in strips to dry for the cold time."

"And skins to dry and cure, to make our warm beds and warm tepees," added Sacagawea.

"And bones to make knives."

"And pointed bones to punch holes."

"And strips of skin for ropes and for sewing."

"We get so many things from the buffalo it is hard to think of them all," said Sacagawea. "If we could have enough buffalo all the time, we would have everything we need and would never be cold or hungry."

"Then why can't we stay here all the time, to get as many as we want?" asked Little Grass.

"The buffalo are not here all the time. They go up that way"—Sacagawea pointed with her left hand to the north—"when the leaves are green. Then when the warm weather is over they come rushing back again, going that way." With her right hand Bird Girl pointed to the south.

Little Grass nodded to show that she understood. "Lots of them?" she asked.

"More than you can imagine. More than the birds. Almost as many as these leaves all around. And when they are running, it sounds like thunder away up in the sky."

"Yes," said Willow Girl, "and you must be careful not to get in their way. They could run over our whole camp, horses and all. The hunters have to work hard, and the horses do, too."

"And don't we work?" asked Little Grass.

"Of course. Hardest of all. The men chase the buffalo and kill them. Then the women cut them up and dry the meat, and cook it—oh, just everything."

"And we *all* eat it," said Little Grass.

"Yes, some of it we eat right away, as soon as we cut up the meat. Some of it we eat when it is cooked, and some after it has been hung up and dried."

"I wish I had some right now," said Little

Grass. "I could eat a lot, anyway, even if I couldn't eat a whole buffalo."

"Look!" said Sacagawea suddenly. "See that!" She pointed to something white and shining beside the trail. It was a buffalo skull, dried and bare, like the one Old Man had set up in the medicine lodge.

She took a small piece from the skull—a tooth—before she remembered that she was no

longer collecting things for Quiet Child's medicine bag. But she tucked it in her belt anyway.

"This is the skull of one of the buffalo we killed last year," she told Little Grass. "That means we are getting near the herds.

"Very soon, maybe in another sleep, we shall pitch our camp where the three rivers come together. Then there will be buffalo nearby, and the hunt will begin."

THE MINITAREES!

AS SOON AS THE TEPEES were put up again in the plain where the rivers met, racks or frames of willow poles had to be made. Sacagawea worked hard helping Mother with this, so that they would be ready when the buffalo were killed. On the racks long strips of buffalo meat would be hung to dry and grow hard.

"You wouldn't think that hard stuff would ever be good to eat," she thought. But then she remembered how good it had tasted before, boiled with berries and roots in a stew, until it was soft again.

One day a group of girls went hunting for some late berries. They went a long distance without finding any.

"Let's climb up on that big rock and see what we can see from there," one of them suggested.

"Do you think we ought to?" asked another.

"Well," said Willow Girl, "no one has told us not to." So up the side of the rock they scrambled. They were out of breath when they reached the top, and were glad to sit and rest for a while.

It was a beautiful sight to see the two rivers coming together off toward the setting sun, and then nearer them the third one joining the others. In a wide stream all three went east together.

"There are *tabba bone* out where that river goes," said Sacagawea.

"But lots of other tribes in between, I have heard," said Willow Girl. "Some we don't even know the names of, and others are our enemies and may come here to fight us."

"Once," said Sacagawea, "I ran off to see where the sun rose in the morning. But as far as I went, it was just as far away as ever."

"It is going to sleep now," said Willow Girl. The girls turned to look at the western mountains. The peaks looked like blue-black clouds where the sun was going down behind them.

"It is time to go back," said one of the older girls. They hurried down the hillside as fast as they could go.

Their mothers looked very serious when the girls came back to the camp.

"We could see you up on the rock," said Willow Girl's mother. "Don't you know that if there were Minitarees coming, they could see you, too? That was a dangerous thing to do."

"Don't you know," Sacagawea's mother said to her, "that when we are buffalo hunting we must do exactly what the hunters say? That is the only way to have a good hunt."

"But we wanted to see how the country looked from up there."

"Others could see you, too. You wouldn't like to be carried off by the Minitarees."

"Why are we so afraid of them?"

"There are many of them, and they are very fierce. They get many shooting-sticks from the pale-faced man, the *tabba bone*. And they are always watching for the Shoshone and trying to take us by surprise."

"Why?"

"They want our horses. There are no horses in the land where the Minitarees come from. They want to take scalps and captives, too."

"What shall we do if they come?"

"We shall have to run and hide in the woods. There are not enough of us to fight them off. Every day our hunters send out scouts in all directions. They will hurry back and tell us if they see any sign of enemies. So you see, when you girls go up high where you can be seen, it is just like telling the enemy where we are. If Bold Hunter were to hear of this, he might not want to pay your father all the horses he has promised."

Sacagawea opened her eyes wide. "Bold Hunter? Promised horses? For what?"

"Why, for you, Bird Girl. He thinks you will make him a good wife. But he will not have enough ponies to give until we have gone back to our mountains and he has made another trip south. There is time enough. You have much yet to learn about being a wife."

Sacagawea felt she was not sorry to wait. Bold Hunter seemed very old to her—almost as old as Father. She would rather stay at home with Mother a long time yet.

After that one forbidden trip the girls were careful to stay closer to the camp. Stories of the fierceness of the Minitarees made them afraid to go far from the others. Besides, they were busy most of the time with the older women.

They worked hard. Even Little Grass had her tasks to do every day. The younger boys, like Little Brother, were freer than she was. But they, too, had to obey rules. They were part of a group with an older boy in charge of them, and felt very important as they went about the camp.

"Everyone works in the buffalo hunt," said Little Brother, "except the babies who are still in their cradleboards."

Sacagawea worked with Mother every day. She learned a great many things. They were all hard to do, but she was glad to learn them. It was hard to cut the heavy buffalo hides and pull them off the big bodies properly. It was hard to cut the meat just right, so that the long thin strips would dry properly. It was hard to remember which of the buffalo's bones could be made into tools, and how to shape them right.

The Shoshone were not only storing up food for the winter ahead. They were storing up work, too. The days sped by while they busied themselves with the buffalo.

The men had the more exciting part. They rode after the great herds of buffalo and shot their arrows or their bullets into the great shaggy beasts. Sacagawea loved to watch Travels Fast ride after them. She was proud of the way he could ride and shoot. He would lean way down on one side of the horse and send his arrow straight to its mark. The buffalo would stagger a few steps farther and then fall to the ground.

"Elder Brother will be a real warrior," Sacagawea said to Mother.

"I would rather he'd be a fast rider," Mother answered, shaking her head. "It is better to get out of the way of the enemy than it is to be wounded or killed."

One morning all the camp was buzzing with work. Sacagawea had just hung some strips of meat up to dry when she saw one of the scouts hurrying in from the east.

"Look, Mother!" she called.

The scout ran in breathlessly. He went straight to Old Man's tepee in the middle of the camp. All the Shoshone could guess what that meant.

"The Minitarees are coming!"

The word went around camp like a flame when the grass is dry. Everyone knew what to expect when Old Man came from his tepee.

Far off the scouts had found signs that a party of Minitarees was on the way. By the signs the scouts could tell of what tribe they were, and how many were coming. They were far more in number than the Shoshone. They were a war and raiding party and were traveling fast, without women or children to hold them back.

"They will be here before the sun is straight overhead!" Old Man warned. "Take what you can and prepare to go at your best speed!"

Almost at the first sight of the scouts the women had begun to pack whatever they could. Most of the things they had worked so hard to prepare must be left behind.

Snatching up what they could carry, the

women and girls plodded behind the men on their horses. In the shortest possible time they were on the way.

They had not gone far when another scout came rushing up. "They are almost upon us!"

"Scatter! To the trees!" The women passed the word along. Quickly they began to run in groups of two or three toward the thicker trees. They had to wade across to the south side of the shallow river to reach shelter.

The men and boys set their horses to galloping. Even so, they were not fast enough. First there were sounds which told them the pursuers were coming nearer. Then bullets began to whine and whistle through the air. More than one horse and rider stumbled and fell.

Sacagawea and Willow Girl were together. With them was Owl Feather, a young woman a few years older. They were on the north side of the stream when the fighting began.

Other women and children had crossed the river and were hurrying to the shelter of the trees on the other side. But the three girls were in plain sight of the Minitarees. They must cross the stream in order to get out of sight.

Sacagawea rushed into the middle of the stream. She heard a little cry and looked back. Willow Girl had just reached the edge of the river when strong brown hands siezed her and threw her to the ground.

Between Sacagawea and the bank Owl Feather slipped on the wet stones. It was easy for the Minitarees to snatch her up and carry her back across the river, where a warrior was guarding Willow Girl.

Sacagawea went on a few more steps.

She was in the strong current of the river now, and it was hard going. The trees on the

south side looked so far away!

Then a strong hand grasped her by the throat. In a moment she, too, was dragged back to the bank where Willow Girl and Owl Feather were held. She was a captive of the Minitarees!

In a few minutes the three girls were being driven back in the direction from which the Minitarees had come. Sacagawea could not understand the language her captors spoke. But she guessed from their actions that they thought there was little use in following the Shoshone any farther.

Instead, they went back to the deserted Shoshone camp. There the Minitarees loaded on their horses all the meat and skins which the girls and their mothers had worked so hard to prepare. It made the girls angry and sick to see all their work going to the enemy.

Then the party was off again. Their captors

made the three girls walk before them, prodded with the whips they used for their horses. Owl Feather had sprained her ankle when she fell. She would not have been able to keep up if Sacagawea and Willow Girl had not helped her. She told the Minitarees she was in pain and begged them to let her walk more slowly. But they paid no attention to her.

"I don't believe they understand a word we say," said Sacagawea.

"I hope they don't," said Willow Girl. "Then we can plan how to get away."

"We can never do that," said Owl Feather, shaking her head sadly. "They will watch us too closely."

"They have to sleep sometime," Willow Girl answered. "I shall be looking for a chance, you may be sure."

That night they were not only watched very

carefully, but were tied up with leather strips. There was no chance to get away. Still Willow Girl did not lose hope.

"If we act as if we don't mind," she said, "they may think we have given up. And in another day they'll think we couldn't tell the way if we tried. But I'll fool them! I'll get back to our people yet."

That second day the girls went along willingly, helping Owl Feather as much as they could. When night came they were not tied up. A big warrior sat beside the fire to guard them, but he proved to be a careless watcher. Perhaps he, too, was tired from the day's long march.

The girls huddled together, very still. The man came over and looked at them closely. He must have thought they were fast asleep, for he went back to the fire and threw himself down. Soon he was sleeping soundly.

So was everyone else, it seemed, except the girls. At length Willow Girl sat up quietly. She whispered to the others, who like her had only been pretending to sleep. "Come on," she said.

It was very dark, but they knew which way to go. They crept off quietly. But after a few steps Owl Feather's foot gave way, and she sank to the ground.

"I'll never make it," she said. The two girls stopped beside her.

"Come on, I'll help you," said Sacagawea.

But Owl Feather shook her head. "I'll only hold you back and we'll get caught. I'll have to stay. But how they will beat me when they find you two are gone!"

"I'll help you get back," said Bird Girl.

"Well, I'm off," said Willow Girl. "I'll wait for you a while, farther on. But if you don't come soon, I'll go on without you. I mean to get back to our people, and after another day's journey we could never make it."

Sacagawea thought for a minute. "They'll beat Owl Feather all the time if there's no one to help her," she said. "I'll stay here with her. Perhaps we can escape later."

Willow Girl squeezed her hand. "I hate to leave you," she said. Then she went off in the dark. Sacagawea helped Owl Feather back to their place.

"We must spread out to look like three instead of two," she whispered. "They mustn't know until morning that Willow Girl is gone." Their watcher stirred as they crept back to their place, but did not come over to look at them.

By and by came a little scuffling sound they had been listening for. It told them that Willow Girl had reached the hobbled horses. With good luck she might catch one to help her escape.

In the morning one Shoshone girl and one horse were missing. The Minitarees scolded Sacagawea and Owl Feather fiercely. After that they kept them under closer guard.

Sacagawea helped Owl Feather and tried not to mind the lashings she got from the whips.

"Anyway," she thought to herself, "I shall see strange places and new people. Perhaps even the *tabba bone*. And wherever we go, the stars will look down on us. They'll be the same kind stars that shone down on us at home."

It was a long, hard journey. When they reached the villages of the Minitarees, Owl Feather's ankle was better, but both girls had sore and bleeding feet. Sacagawea's dress had been torn by the thorny bushes. Her back was sore from the whip that had lashed her so often. But she held her head up, and her brown eyes looked about, seeing everything.

The two girls sat together while the women of the village prepared the feast that would celebrate the victorious return of the Minitaree warriors.

"Look," said Owl Feather. "That man is different from the rest! He has blue eyes, and his skin isn't really brown."

"He must be a *tabba bone*," Sacagawea whispered. They both watched the strange man very closely. They heard the Indians call him something that sounded like "Shobbono."

He was playing a game with some of the men and they were all laughing. But the white man laughed longest and hardest. He seemed to be winning, for the pile of skins beside him grew higher as he and the others played.

He looked over at the two captives, then rose and walked toward them, motioning for them to stand up. He looked Owl Feather over

carefully, pinched her arm and looked at her hands to see if they showed signs of work.

"Here!" he cried to the others. "I need a woman to take care of my pelts for me. I'll buy this one!"

Owl Feather turned to Sacagawea and threw her arms about her, gazing up defiantly at the white man. She could not speak a word that he could understand. Nevertheless, she made it quite plain to him that she and Sacagawea must not be separated.

Sacagawea held out her smaller hands, to show that they, too, were working hands. The man laughed aloud.

"All right," he said. "The two of them, then! Me, Toussaint Charbonneau, I shall have two squaws in my lodge. But yes, they shall do much work for me!"

Owl Feather cried a little when they were taken off to the white man's lodge, but Sacagawea comforted her. "We can help each other and maybe he will not be too bad to us."

And to herself she thought: "This is the strangest thing that has ever happened to me. None of my people ever saw a *tabba bone*. I myself never saw one of them till today, and now I belong to one of them!"

FIVE YEARS LATER

FIVE COLD WINTERS had gone by since Sacagawea and Owl Feather had been carried away. In all that time no word had come to the Shoshone about the captured girls.

There had been rejoicing when Willow Girl came back, a few days after the capture. There was rejoicing in the midst of sorrow for those who had been killed or stolen by the enemy. But of Sacagawea and Owl Feather, Willow Girl could only say that they must have gone on with the Minitarees.

Five years later, Willow Woman was very busy with a husband and a tepee to take care of. Even Little Grass was growing up to be a young woman. They often spoke of Bird Girl and wondered what had happened to her.

One morning Little Grass was picking berries in a small ravine, or valley. With her were an older woman and a little girl. It was late summer. Soon it would be time for the Shoshone to gather for their yearly buffalo hunt.

Suddenly Little Grass heard a strange sound. She looked off in the direction her people traveled when they went to hunt buffalo. Her eyes widened with astonishment. Three strange men were coming toward them.

At the sight of them, Little Grass dashed off and hid in the underbrush. The woman and girl were caught too quickly to hide. They stood still with their heads bowed, expecting the men to kill them or drag them away.

In a few moments, however, Little Grass was surprised to hear the older woman calling her.

"Come on out, Little Grass!" she cried. "These men are friends! They are *tabba bone*! They have gifts for us!"

And it was true. How proud Little Grass was that evening to tell Willow Woman and the other women and girls about it!

"See these bright round things with holes in them! I can string them together and wear them about my neck. See this flat shiny thing! When I look into it I see another girl looking back at me! See the red spots on my cheeks! The white man painted them there to show us that he is friendly."

"And you brought the *tabba bone* back to us?" one woman asked.

"First we brought them to the warriors, who

were happy to see them. Then we all came together to the council lodge."

"And they say there are more of them coming?" another woman asked.

"Yes, a band of them is coming up the river. We go tomorrow to meet them."

In the morning when the Shoshone went to meet the strangers, there was the greatest surprise of all. For among the white soldiers was a young Indian woman!

She was looking from one to the other of the Shoshone as if she were searching for a familiar face. It was Willow Woman who first recognized her.

"Sacagawea!" They rushed toward each other, laughing and crying at the same time.

Here was the long-lost Shoshone girl, and with her a pale-faced husband and a baby!

Here was Willow Woman's lost friend and

playmate. The two hugged each other. At first they could scarcely speak for happiness.

The thirty white men were United States soldiers. Their leaders were Captains Meriwether Lewis and William Clark, whom President Jefferson had sent to find a way across the continent to the Pacific Ocean. White men called this the Lewis and Clark Expedition. It was the year 1805.

"They are kind, and they are brave, these two captains," Sacagawea told the Shoshone. "They say that the Indians should all be at peace. They did not come on this long journey to fight."

"Where did they come from?" asked her listeners.

"From far to the east. They came up the big river. When it froze they stopped and built themselves winter lodges near the homes of the Mandans and Minitarees, where we live.

"When spring came and they traveled on
again, my husband and I came with them."

"Your husband is a *tabba bone,* too," said Little
Grass, "but he seems different from the captains.
How is that?"

"There are different tribes among the pale-faced
ones, just as with us. The captains and their men

are called Americans. My husband is called French. He bought me from the Minitarees long ago, and now we are husband and wife. He came along to interpret—to change into other language—what the American captains have to say to us. I have learned some of their words, too, and I shall have to help in the telling."

"Even now," another woman spoke up, "the great medicine lodge is being made ready for the council."

"But where are all your tepees?" asked Bird Woman.

"Ah, that is so sad a story! Our enemies from the west attacked us four moons ago. They drove us from our tepees and carried them off. Many of our bravest warriors were killed. So we built these brush shelters, until we can go to the buffalo grounds to get more skins."

The women had even sadder news to tell

Sacagawea. Both her father and her mother had been killed. Only her two brothers were left.

"Our head men," said Willow Woman, "were all killed or captured. Now young Cameathwait is our leader. It is he whose words you will help to interpret in the council chamber."

"Cameathwait? That means 'one who never walks.' Then you have plenty of horses?" asked Sacagawea.

"Yes, many of them."

"Our party"—Sacagawea spoke proudly of the *tabba bone*—"our party wants to trade with you for horses. Canoes can no longer travel up the little stream. They will need horses to carry the goods over the high hills and far to the big western waters."

"But you will stay here with us, won't you?" asked Little Grass. "Remember your father promised you to Bold Hunter."

"I am the wife of Toussaint Charbonneau," answered Bird Woman. "Bold Hunter will not want me when he knows I have a pale-faced husband and a baby whose skin is lighter than my own. Did you ever see such a fine baby?"

"Ah-ah," said the women. "A fine baby, indeed, and with a *tabba bone* for his father."

"As for me," Sacagawea went on, "I shall go on to the setting sun with my husband and the party of Americans."

"Ah-ah!" There were little cries and murmurs of surprise among the listening women. "How daring is our Bird Woman!"

Sacagawea was wondering to herself which one of the young men she had known might be Cameathwait, "one who never walks." All the young men changed their names when they became warriors. Evidently this warrior had been named for his skill in capturing horses.

She went into the council house modestly, her eyes on the ground, as was fitting for a woman who was permitted to come into the council. She heard the captains make their first speech. Then her husband repeated it in the language of the Minitarees. She herself listened to the Minitaree talk and repeated it in the Shoshone language, so that all the Shoshone might understand.

The young chief began to make an answer. Something in his voice sounded familiar. She lifted her eyes to his face. Then she gave a little cry and rushed up to him, laughing and weeping at the same time. She flung her blanket over his shoulder, and they stood with their arms about each other. He was almost as excited as she was. For a moment they quite forgot the council and the people about them.

Cameathwait, the leader, was Bird Woman's own beloved Elder Brother!

For as many days as one could count on both hands, the American party and the Shoshone stayed together. Cameathwait was anxious to take his people on the buffalo hunt. He even made plans to slip away in the night, leaving the *tabba bone*.

But Sacagawea heard the women whispering of these plans. She knew how badly the Shoshone needed the buffalo skins for the tepees and the buffalo meat for their food. She had never forgotten the old hungry time in the mountains.

But she understood, too, how badly the white men needed to buy Shoshone horses for their journey over the mountains. They had come up the Missouri River, as they called it, until their heavily loaded canoes could no longer be paddled in the shallow water. Now they must have horses to carry the canoe loads across to the river that flowed to the west. When they reached the western river, they would make other boats to paddle down the stream.

Sacagawea wanted them to carry out their plans. She wanted to go on to the great western water which she had heard about so long ago. She went to Captain Lewis before evening came.

"My brother," she told him, "is eager to slip away. He is planning to leave you tonight. He has sent word to the camps to break up and be ready to go."

Captain Lewis called Cameathwait and two other young leaders to talk with him. They smoked the friendly peace pipe, and then Lewis asked why they were planning to run away and leave him without horses.

"If you wish our friendship," he told them, "you will tell your people to stay here until our trading is done."

The two other leaders said Cameathwait alone had made the plans to go off. At first Cameathwait did not know what to say. Then he told them that his people were in too great need to stay any longer. In the end, however, he agreed to stay until the trading was finished.

At last the trading was finished. The white men had horses to carry their goods and Shoshone guides to lead them over the mountains. It was the loyalty of Bird Woman that had made this possible, Captain Lewis declared.

He had given Charbonneau goods with which to buy a horse for Sacagawea. When the expedition went on to the west, Bird Woman rode proudly on a good horse, as she had dreamed of doing when she first tried to ride Star.

Just before they left, Little Grass came running up with something in her hand. Sacagawea

looked at it and recognized Quiet Child and the small medicine bag. They looked torn and trampled, but they were really her own.

"I found this," Little Grass said, "when the enemies had torn down your mother's tepee. Is it yours? Willow Woman thought it was."

"It is," Sacagawea answered. She drew the string of the bag Grandmother had helped her make so long ago. "And see here!" She took out the things she had used when she played that Quiet Child was a medicine woman.

"See the bright feathers," said Little Grass. "How pretty they are!"

"Look up there!" said Sacagawea suddenly. Over their heads floated the red, white, and blue flag of the United States.

"See! This one is like the red stripes—like the good fire that warms us in the cold. Here is the lovely white—like the snow that shines on the top of the mountains. And here is the beautiful blue sky in which the stars are shining."

"You did not know, when you gathered them!" whispered Little Grass. Her eyes were wide with amazement.

"No, I did not know. But it must have been a sign of what was going to happen to me. Keep these things, Little Grass, and look at them to remind yourself of the American country and its red, white, and blue flag. It will tell you the Americans are friends to the Shoshone, and the Shoshone should always be friendly to them."

After saying good-bye, the Shoshone turned their horses to the east, toward the buffalo grounds along the Missouri River.

All the way they talked about their visitors. Most of all they talked about Sacagawea, their Bird Woman. It seemed strange to some of them that she had not wanted to stay with her own people. But to those who knew her best it was not surprising at all.

"Even when she was little," said Willow Woman to Little Grass, "she was always wanting to see new places. She was not afraid of new things, as so many of us are."

"Do you remember," said Little Grass, "that she used to say someday she would have a horse of her own? How happy she was to ride away on one of our best horses. Her husband bought it for her."

"But the captains," said another woman, "gave him the beads and mirrors to buy it with."

"Those captains!" said Willow Woman. "She says they are always kind, brave warriors, too. The tall redheaded one, she told me, saved her life one day when a great flood of water came suddenly down the hillside. It would have washed her and her baby away if he had not pulled her to a safe place."

"And now she is going to see where the salmon come from into the big rivers," Little Grass spoke up.

"Yes," replied her sister, "that is something else she was always wanting to see. She thinks they will stay for the next cold time near that great salty water."

"There are many enemies on the way," Little Grass objected. "How will such a small party get that far?"

"She says the *tabba bone* are friends to all Indians of all tribes, and they ask them to be friendly with one another."

"Could that ever be?" asked Little Grass.

"I do not know. But after this I believe the Shoshone will always be friendly to the *tabba bone* because they have been so kind to us, and to our own Bird Woman!"

At the head of the traveling Shoshone rode Cameathwait. Soon they were joined by the hunting party of which Younger Brother was a member. The hunter brother heard with surprise of the visit of the American explorers.

"We could scarcely speak," Cameathwait told him, "when we saw the young woman who had come all the long way with them. It was truly our own sister, our Bird Girl. And away with them she went, riding a good horse, while men walked."

"And she has a pale-faced husband? And traveling with all those men?" The younger brother could scarcely believe such a strange story.

"Yes, she says they mean to keep on until they reach the Great Wide Water, where the sun goes down. Then, after the cold time, they will journey back again. They will go north of our country until they reach the villages of the Mandans. That is where they started."

"And will the white men stay at those Mandan villages, too?" asked Younger Brother.

"Oh, no, they live much farther on. They have more villages than anyone can count, she says. But she and her husband will stay with the Mandans, while the others will go on down the big river to their homes."

"What are they coming so far for?"

"To see the country and the Indian tribes. Our sister says they will tell them all to be at peace with one another. For all of them they have presents, like the things they gave us, and for each of them a flag which they say means peace and friendliness."

"Do you think we shall ever see these *tabba bone* again, brother?"

"If there are so many, it seems to me that others will come after these we have seen. And I think we must be friends with them, because our sister has found them so good."

"So she likes the *tabba bone* well?" asked the younger brother.

"Well—very well. She would not stay with us, though the women pleaded with her. But she was ever one for adventure, and never afraid. She will travel with the white men all the way. The enemy tribes beyond us will know it is a friendly group, because a woman and a child are along."

"It is a fine thing."

"Yes, it is," agreed Cameathwait. "If the custom were the same for women as it is for men, we would give her a new name—perhaps one like Woman Warrior. And we shall always tell of her now, in our dances."

THE LONG
JOURNEY ENDS

ONE AUGUST DAY in the year 1806 several canoes came gliding swiftly down the Missouri River. They had come from beyond the Shining Mountains far to the west and were going downstream to the villages of the Mandan Indians. There were thirty-one men, one woman, and one baby boy in the canoes.

The two leading canoes carried the captains of the party. One was Meriwether Lewis.

The other was friendly, red-haired William Clark. The woman was Sacagawea, and the baby was her son, whom Captain Clark called Pomp. They were riding with Sacagawea's husband, Charbonneau, in Captain Clark's canoe.

Captain Lewis was riding in the canoe just ahead.

The long journey upon which Captains Lewis and Clark led their men was drawing to an end. Little Pomp was nineteen months old. He had been less than two months old when the party had left the Mandan villages. During all those months he had journeyed with the others to the Pacific Ocean and back again.

As the canoes glided down the river, Sacagawea was thinking about the journey. She remembered the things they had seen and the adventures they had had. Her heart beat faster when she recalled her own people, the Shoshone, and her meeting with Willow Woman and her dear Elder Brother. But she was not sorry that she had left them again to go with her husband and the *tabba bone*.

With two of Sacagawea's people to guide

them, the white men had crossed the mountains by twisting, difficult trails and had come at last to the Snake River. Here they had made friends among the Chopunnish or Nez Percé Indians.

They did not need horses now, so they left them with the Nez Percés and built more canoes. Sacagawea remembered those days of the canoe-building well. The food of the Nez Percés did not agree with the white men and many of them had fallen ill.

At last the canoes were ready, however, and the party set out. Down the Snake River they had gone until they reached the great Columbia River. And down the Columbia, past rapids and waterfalls, they had gone until they reached the sea. There, near the river's mouth, they had spent the winter.

It had been a mild winter, but very rainy. To protect themselves from the rain they had built a fort, which they called Fort Clatsop. Clatsop was the name of a friendly tribe of Indians that lived near by.

At first the people of the expedition had camped on the north side of the river, but they put the fort on the south side. There they had more protection from heavy winds and storms, and the game was more plentiful. The fort contained seven small cabins surrounded by a log wall.

Sacagawea smiled again as she thought of Fort Clatsop and the chief of the Clatsop tribe. This old man was a great favorite of the two captains. He often came to visit the fort. Sometimes he brought food to sell or to give to the party, and sometimes he came only in the hope that he would be given a present.

When the party left in the spring to return home, they had given him the fort. He was delighted. "It will be our home during the rainy season," he had said.

One thing about Fort Clatsop had disappointed Sacagawea. Even though the river had been wide here, she had not been able to see the ocean, the great stinking water that stretched without end toward the setting sun.

Some of the men had been sent to the ocean to make salt from its water. But Sacagawea and her husband were not of this party. It would be sad indeed, Sacagawea thought, to be so near the great water and not really see it.

By and by the saltmakers sent word that a great fish had been washed up on shore. This fish was as long as a tree is tall, the men said. They called it a whale. The two captains gave some of the men permission to go to see the whale.

When she heard about the great fish,

Sacagawea could wait no longer. It took a great deal of courage for her to ask anything of Captain Clark. He had always been her friend and had always liked to play with little Pomp. Nevertheless, he was one of the captains, and when one of the captains spoke everyone did as he said. But somehow Sacagawea found the courage to approach him.

"It seems hard to me," she had said, "that I should come so far and then have no chance to see the great water and the big fish."

Captain Clark had been kind, as he always was. "You shall go, Janey," he promised. He called her Janey because her name was long and hard to pronounce. And so the Charbonneaus went with the party to see the dead whale and the ocean.

By the time they had reached the sea, only the skeleton of the great fish remained. Indians

from miles around had come and carried away
its flesh. But Sacagawea could tell from the
curving bones how large the creature had been.

Even now her eyes grew wide with amazement
as she thought about it. Could she ever make the
Mandan women believe that she had seen such
a thing? It seemed unreal even to herself now as
she glided down the muddy river, past cottonwood trees and the brown plains beyond them.

It would be hard to make the Mandan
women believe her stories about the ocean, too,

she knew. Years ago she had promised herself that she would see the ocean some day, and finally she had. She had stood at its very edge and watched the waves curl up on the sandy beach and break and draw back again. She had breathed deeply of the salty air and had looked far out across the water. As far as she could see there was only water.

How could she find words to tell the Mandan women about that? What could she say that they would understand or believe? All they knew was the river and the grassy plain with its vast herds of buffalo. Could she compare the ocean with the plain that rolled on and on until it met the sky?

The canoe shuddered slightly as it struck a hidden log. Sacagawea looked quickly down at the little boy playing at her feet in the bottom of the canoe. Then she smiled.

"You have seen the whale and the ocean, too," she said. "You are too little to remember them now. But I shall tell you some day how you stood on the sand and patted the waves with your hands and laughed with pleasure. You were just learning to walk, but you were not afraid of the waves or the bitter water."

All these things had happened during the rainy winter. Since then, spring had come and gone and summer as well was almost gone. Now in August the party was nearing the Mandan villages and Sacagawea was almost home. She and her husband would say good-bye to the Americans there.

When the party camped for the night, Captain Lewis and Captain Clark sat talking before the fire. Captain Clark was watching Sacagawea play with her baby.

"What a fine traveling companion our Janey

has been!" he said. "I don't know what we would have done without her. We expected her to help get horses from the Shoshone because she knew their language. It was sheer good fortune to find that her brother was chief of the tribe."

"Even so, he would have slipped away from us if she had not told us about his plans," Captain Lewis pointed out.

"Yes, she has been very loyal to us," said Captain Clark. "But most important of all, she has helped us just by being who she is. How could any of us grumble about hardships when we have seen her toiling along patiently day after day without complaining?"

"And always carrying Pomp on her back!"

Captain Clark laughed. "You know, Pomp has helped us, too, in a way. The very fact that we had a woman and baby with us showed that we were a peaceful group. No group of warriors would take along a woman and her child if they intended to fight."

"I suppose we can thank Sacagawea and Pomp for protecting us," Captain Lewis said.

"And for many other things as well," Clark added. "President Jefferson will be grateful to her for saving our records and journals the day the canoe turned over."

"I can see her now," Lewis said with a laugh. "When the canoe turned over, Charbonneau started to squeal with fright. But Janey paddled around calmly, catching everything she could reach before the current carried it away."

"Do you remember the time in the mountains when game was hard to find and our provisions were almost gone? She gave us a handful of flour that she had saved for her baby."

"She showed us how to find roots in places where the gophers had hidden them, too."

"She tells me her people are often hungry," said Captain Clark. "They did not have much when we met them in the mountains. I don't know what they would have done without the things we gave them."

"Still, they couldn't understand why she wanted to go on with us." Lewis thought for a moment. "I wish we had named something more than a creek for her," he went on. "But at any rate, you gave the baby's name to the biggest rock we saw on the whole journey."

"Little Pomp will have no reason to complain about his pillar. You know, if that boy has half the alertness and dependability of his mother, he'll be worth watching. I'd like to send him to school some day."

A day or two later the canoes reached the Mandan villages. There was great rejoicing among the Mandans and the Minitarees over the party's return. There was also great rejoicing in the lodge of Toussaint Charbonneau, where Owl Feather had waited patiently for Sacagawea and Charbonneau to return.

Sacagawea was happy to see Owl Feather, but at the same time she was sad. Soon the Americans would be going down the river to their own country and she would never see them again. Never again would Captain Clark call her Janey or laughingly play with little Pomp. Sacagawea knew that she would miss that.

But there was a surprise in store for her. One evening, shortly before the Americans were to leave, Captain Clark made a visit to the Charbonneau lodge.

"Charbonneau," he said, "would you like to come to St. Louis with me? You know how much I like Pomp. I would like to give him a good

education. If you come, I will buy you a farm."

Sacagawea looked hopefully at her husband. Perhaps she could still see the huge villages of which Captain Clark and the others had told her!

Charbonneau shook his head. "Thank you, Captain," he said, "but I am a trader and trapper, not a farmer. I shall stay here with the life that I know."

Sacagawea lowered her eyes and said nothing.

"And the boy?" asked Captain Clark. "What about him?"

Charbonneau looked at Sacagawea. She lifted her head. "When the child is old enough he will come," she said. "I give you my word."

"I'll be waiting for him, Janey. And I'll take good care of him for you, too." With a friendly smile, Captain Clark turned and left the lodge, with Charbonneau close behind him.

Alone, Sacagawea looked at Pomp sadly. The

adventure was over now. She had gone back to her Shining Mountains and beyond them to the great river and the bitter lake without end. Now she was back among the Mandans and Minitarees, and her white friends were getting ready to leave.

"Well," she thought, "I can still tell the people here of the things I have seen. They may not believe me, but how can I blame them? It seems strange even to me that I have done so many of the things I dreamed about as a girl up in the Shining Mountains."

A few days later she stood on the bank of the river, watching the canoes start on their downward journey. She felt sad as she watched the men take their places in the canoes. She had spent so many months with them, had undergone so many hardships with them! It was almost as if she were saying good-bye to her own brothers.

The lead canoe, carrying Captain Clark, set out. He turned to wave, and Sacagawea waved in return and held Pomp up to see. Then one by one the rest of the canoes set out.

The current was swift and the canoes grew smaller in the distance. Soon they went around a bend in the river and Sacagawea saw them no more.

Today in Bismarck, the capital of North Dakota, there stands a statue of an Indian mother and child. It was placed there to honor Sacagawea. Bismarck is farther down the Missouri River than the spot where the villages of the Mandan Indians stood. Nevertheless, it is a fitting place to remind people of the famous journey which this remarkable young Indian woman made so many years ago.

Almost at the other end of the long journey,

on a wooded hillside in a park in Portland, Oregon, stands another statue of Bird Woman and her baby boy. The money for this statue was given by women and children who lived in many different parts of the country and who belonged to many different races. They all wanted to honor this young Indian woman who had served the United States so well.

All across the country, from North Dakota to Oregon, there are reminders of the famous journey which the seventeen-year-old wife and mother made. There is a creek bearing her name. Until recent years there was a high rock which Captain Clark called Pompey's Pillar, in honor of Sacagawea's little boy. There are rivers, mountains, and lakes whose names were given to them by Lewis and Clark.

Sacagawea would be greatly surprised today if she could see these statues and markers. She would find it hard to understand why the people of the United States have taken the trouble to remember and honor her.

But then, it would be hard for her to understand how important the Lewis and Clark Expedition was. And it would even be harder for her to understand how important she herself was to the expedition's success.

Lewis and Clark were the first white men ever to reach the Pacific Ocean from the eastern part of our country. By doing so, they had proved that it was possible to go from the Atlantic Ocean to the Pacific Ocean by land. For a long time men tried to find a water route across the continent. Now, by making their successful journey, Lewis and Clark had shown that such a route was not needed.

They had traveled all the way from St. Louis to the headwaters of the Missouri River, which

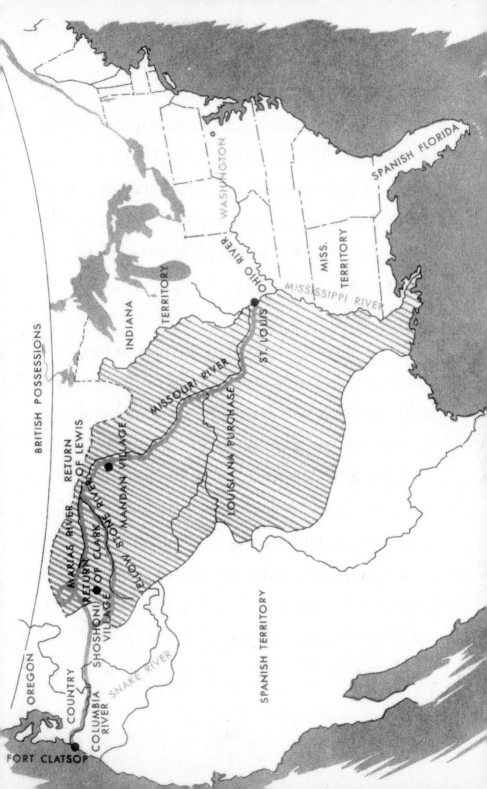

SPANISH FLORIDA

WASHINGTON

OHIO RIVER

MISSISSIPPI RIVER

MISS.
TERRITORY

ST. LOUIS

INDIANA

TERRITORY

MISSOURI RIVER

LOUISIANA PURCHASE

BRITISH POSSESSIONS

RETURN OF LEWIS

MARIAS RIVER

RETURN OF CLARK

YELLOWSTONE RIVER

MANDAN VILLAGE

SPANISH TERRITORY

SHOSHONI VILLAGE

OREGON

COUNTRY

COLUMBIA RIVER

SNAKE RIVER

FORT CLATSOP

no white man had ever seen. They had crossed the Rocky Mountains and floated down the Snake and Columbia rivers to the Pacific Ocean, through country which no white man had ever seen. Then they had retraced their steps, up the Columbia and Snake rivers, across the mountains, and down the Missouri again.

It had been a hard journey, requiring great courage and strength, but they had made it safely and without trouble. Furthermore, they had carried a message of peace and friendship to many tribes of Indians that had never seen a white man before. They had made friends of some tribes, such as the Shoshone, who were always to remain friendly to the United States.

Forty years later their journey was one reason that the United States could claim ownership of the "Oregon country." That was what the land beyond the Rocky Mountains came to be called. Washington, Oregon, Idaho, Montana, and Wyoming are all part of the United States today because of the Lewis and Clark Expedition. It was the courage and persistence of the two captains and their twenty-eight men that brought this about.

But if the American people owe much to these men, in a way they owe even more to Sacagawea. The party happened to travel through the country that she knew best. But she was not merely a guide, as many people have said. Even more, she was an interpreter and a kind of ambassador of good will.

She translated the words of the white men not only to the Shoshone but to many tribes that lived beyond them as well. Wherever there were Shoshone prisoners or others who understood the Shoshone language, Sacagawea carried the white men's words.

Sometimes these words would be translated into five or six languages before they reached the tribe for whom they were meant. It was Sacagawea's quick thinking and ready tongue that brought this about.

As an ambassador or messenger of good will she was equally important, if not more important. What Indian tribe could fail to think well of the white men when she was so well treated by them and so happy to be with them? They must be good men, the Indians felt, if they were so kind to an Indian woman and her baby.

Her presence proved that the white men were peaceful, too. Among the Indians, war parties never took women and children along. When they saw Sacagawea, the Indians knew that Lewis and Clark wanted only to be their friends.

Sacagawea would truly be surprised if she could know how highly she is honored today.

She was a modest woman who thought herself of little importance. She had ambitious dreams of seeing things which the rest of her people had never seen. She had dreams of doing things which the rest of them had never done. But she never dreamed that her name would one day become a symbol of bravery, endurance, and wholehearted loyalty.